SECRETS OF THE SLEEPER

True Nature Series Book One

Karen Lynn Bennett

What If Press
San Jose, California

This is a work of fiction. Names, characters, organizations, places, events, and incidents are either products of the author's imagination or are used fictitiously.

Copyright ©2016 by Karen Lynn Bennett
All Rights Reserved.
10202016

Published by What If Press.

No part of this publication may be reproduced, distributed or transmitted in any form or by any means, including photocopying, recording, or other electronic or mechanical methods, without the prior written permission of the publisher, except in the case of brief quotations embodied in critical reviews and certain other noncommercial uses permitted by copyright law.

karenlynnbennett.com

Cover design by oliviaprodesign
Book Layout ©2013 BookDesignTemplates.com

Secrets of the Sleeper/ Karen Lynn Bennett. – 2nd ed.
ISBN 978-0-9977867-1-2

To my greatest supporters
Edward, Lauren, and Brenna

"Even a soul submerged in sleep
is hard at work and helps
make something of the world."

– ***HERACLITUS, FRAGMENTS***

Prologue

Lydia Parker

Ten Months ago

"I CAN'T BELIEVE YOU did that! I hate you right now!"

My daughter's words echoed in my head as I turned the car toward downtown. I wanted to talk about it, but I knew I would be wasting my breath until she calmed down.

So, I ignored Tru, who fumed in the backseat, preferring to sit as far away from me as possible. I imagined what she was thinking: *I have the most overprotective mother on the planet! You embarrassed me in front of all my friends! I'm the only person in my entire school who isn't at that party.*

I took a deep breath and unclenched my hands from the steering wheel. Getting angry was not going to help, and neither was feeling guilty. Sure, I knew the parents of the girl who threw the party. Sure, they seemed like a nice family. But, if I had learned anything during my forty years as a schoolteacher, it was that families were more than they appeared on the outside, and that really weird stuff happened in the "nice" families as often as it did in the more suspect ones. Didn't Tru watch the news? Every time I turned it on, another kid had gone missing, another college student had overdosed—and worse. I thought she had more sense. Besides, I had told Tru that she couldn't go, and she had gone anyway. She knew the consequences and now she was grounded. Parents had to follow through with their rules. Kids needed boundaries. I loved my daughter, and even though it meant being the enemy for the moment, I would not let her down like my parents had my sister.

Caroline. That was another reason I wanted to keep Tru close right now. Who was I kidding? It superseded all the other reasons.

I could not believe Caroline was back from the dead. It had been over ten years since she had died. Since I *thought* she died. And Caroline was different, in a bad way. She seemed scattered and paranoid. We'd met in private and Caroline insisted that I swear on our mother's grave not to tell anyone about her. She said it was better if everyone thought she was dead. Who was she running from?

Perhaps the most jarring difference was how young my sister looked. I was sixty-five and ten years older than my sister, but Caroline had looked as young as the last time I'd seen her—over twenty years ago! I almost didn't believe it was Caroline. But then she had talked about things only my sister would know.

That's when I decided she was doing drugs. Yet... What if she was in some kind of pharmaceutical drug experiment? With Caroline, it could be anything.

And the things she had said. They were fantastical! Caroline had truly lost it. She rambled about her baby dying, about being "collected," about someone forcing her to fix people, and running away. And then she said she had secrets, many secrets. Well, obviously! I wasn't sure I wanted to know any of her secrets. I definitely didn't want her anywhere near my family. Caroline was certifiable.

But, as her only remaining relative how could I turn her away? I bit my lip, feelings of remorse crumbling my resolve. No, I wouldn't feel guilty. Straightening my shoulders, I found the metal spine I was known for. I had acted in good faith and I wasn't going to ruin another life trying to fix one that was already too far-gone.

Somewhere in my conversation with Caroline, I remembered Uriel, her odd husband whom I had met only once or twice. When I asked if he was alive, too, she shook her head. Uriel was dead. Frankly, I didn't know what to believe. Then Caroline followed that news by telling me there was a new man in her life. That she loved him. That he was her other half, or some malarkey like that.

But I knew my sister to be flighty and mercurial. She had drifted from one catastrophe to another her whole life. Now it was up to me to figure out what to do with her. Tonight I would tell James. I pressed a hand into my chest, feeling my heartburn start up. Or was it guilt? I should have told him already, but some part of me had wanted to believe in my sister. Now Caroline wanted to meet again, secretly. It had to stop. I would be enabling Caroline if I allowed this to go on. Besides, if she figured out—well, no, that just wasn't an option. I shuddered at the thought. The next time we met, James would come with me. We would convince her to go to the hospital. That's just how it would have to be.

With my decision made, I felt much of my earlier tension evaporate and realized I had almost reached my next stop. Downtown. I cracked the car window, allowing the night air to drift in. It had been a short drive from the party. One of the perks of living where we did.

I loved the sleepy little town of Scotts Valley. It was close enough to the ocean, but far enough away from the famous beach town of Santa Cruz that I didn't have to deal with too many tourists. It was a family town in the middle of the Santa Cruz Mountains, and its constant smell of pine and redwood infiltrated the car, refreshing me, regenerating me as it always did. I pulled over to park along the street across from a coffee shop.

"Tru, I'm just stopping to grab some newspapers for tomorrow's class. I'm subbing for Mrs. Alvarez. She's out on maternity leave."

There was no response, and I sighed. "I'll only be a minute." Parenting had its drawbacks. Tonight, for instance. Disciplining was the worst part, in my opinion, but Tru was worth all the stress. One day she would understand.

I started across the street toward a newspaper machine hoping to find a few papers left in it. I didn't want to prolong this little field trip more than necessary. Even from the backseat Tru's anger slammed into me like furious ocean waves. It would be good to get home to James. It wouldn't be the first time he played the buffer between Tru and me.

Just as I reached the middle of the road, a car roared around the corner, its lights blinding me.

"No—"

1

It

Tru Parker

Today

"Alondrea!"

A ghostly plea, with the intangibility of a dream within a dream, induced a stabbing panic like I'd never felt before. It sounded far away, perhaps over that hill—the one I could barely make out through the smoky haze filtering through the thick trees. My heart pounded to one thought—

Dan-ger-Dan-ger.

"A-lon-dre-a!"

It was a woman's voice, a terrified voice, and it was fading along with the clear blue sky above. I wanted that voice, and the woman it belonged to, but my mind was like the smoke slipping between the pine needles above me, unable to grasp the moment. I began to cough.

A dog howled, a ghostly entreaty echoing through my confusion. Fright stepped back as hope pushed forward. But a child's hitched sobbing pulled me up short. Heavy paws thumped toward the small form. The dog...no...not a dog...a wolf opened up its toothy mouth and reached for—

My scream must have woken up Dad, because as I shrunk away from the image in my dream, I heard him say, "Tru! Wake up!"

Suddenly I was back in my bed, legs twisted in the blankets, and Dad clutching me to his chest.

"Hey there, Tru Lee, I've got you."

I breathed in his familiar scent, and sighed. I thanked God that my dad smelled of chocolate instead of mothballs like Principal Millard—aka "Mothballs Millard." And even though Dad's embrace was the same as the million or so preceding hugs I'd received from him over my sixteen years, these days I treasured each one so much more than I ever did, even more than Mummy, my stuffed animal that I'd had for as long as I could remember and which I still tucked into bed with me each night.

"They're starting again, Tru Lee." His hand gently rubbed my back. "I think we could use some expert help here."

The gruffly whispered words scratched at the ball of remorse I kept locked away, just as his rough whiskers chafed my cheek, but they didn't hurt, not like his words. I knew where this conversation was going.

"No!" I denied, intending to say it softly but unable to do so. It was more of a choking bark. I pulled abruptly out of his embrace and glared at him.

"I don't want to talk to some psycho shrink! It was just a stupid nightmare! Geez."

I instantly regretted it. He was trying so hard, and here I was, becoming that girl—that spoiled, selfish girl I swore I was never going to be again. But I couldn't seem to stop hurting the people who loved me the most.

"Tru, what you're feeling is normal. You shouldn't feel bad about talking to a specialist. I really think you just need to discuss it with *someone.*"

It. That word encompassed so much. Did we even have the same definition of *It?* Doubtful. I closed my eyes, searching my mind frantically for a better argument than the snarky comment about to bust out of my mouth. *Look him in the eyes*, I thought. He couldn't take my direct eye contact without backing down.

"I can't, Dad—" I opened my eyes and froze, losing my train of thought. A raw, red scratch ran down the side of his weathered face.

I did that. Ah, man! I was such a loser.

I pretended that I didn't see it—normal people wouldn't see it. It was too dark. He let go of me and stood up, his gray hair sticking up all over the place. He looked old and worn out standing there in his wrinkled pajamas, and I felt a fresh wave of shame. *I* put those wrinkles on his face, that gray in his hair.

Taking a deep breath, I softened my voice. "I'm fine. Just a dream. No biggie. I'm going back to sleep. Big day tomorrow, you know."

He pursed his lips, staring at me. I held my ground.

With a sigh, he relented. "Okay, kiddo." He leaned in and kissed my forehead, unknowingly branding me a liar. I felt awful lying to him and I imagined a red letter "L" for liar bright and glaring on my forehead. I itched to rub it away but just mumbled good night and burrowed into my pillow. The mattress sprang back up as he stumbled toward the door, tripping over the land mines of clothes piled here and there.

I mumbled a "Sorry," to which he said for the hundredth time, "You need to clean up this place." He didn't realize I was saying sorry for something else.

The door closed a second later.

Lifting my head for a second to peer at the clock on my dresser, I saw the glowing red numbers: 3:30 a.m. Why me? I tried to untwist my legs from the sticky sheets, but they held tight. Ugh! I kicked harder, gritting my teeth, battling the clingy sheets with panic. A few more angry flicks of my legs, and I was free. I shoved the sheets to the floor, trouncing them in retaliation. Giving them one last scowl, I muttered my way over to my window and ripped back my curtains. With a quick yank at the window, cool air flowed freely into the room. Goose bumps appeared all over my feverish skin. Ahh. I backed up to the middle of my room, pressing my hands against the sides of my face, rubbing my temples.

I didn't want this to happen, not today. I needed to...to...what did I need? I felt disoriented, angry that I still wasn't fixed, and guilty about my inability to make things easier for Dad. I was a bit of a mess.

Oh, I remembered. I needed to *not* look like crap on the first day of school.

I glanced toward my mirrored closet doors. Yeah, it was bad. Puffy brown eyes, pale cheeks, and hair clinging to my sweaty face. Long blond strands hung in tangles to the middle of my back. Great, looked like I needed to wash it again, with a whole bottle of conditioner. It was a Halloween wig gone wild.

The meager glow from the moon outside my window failed to illuminate the room; however, I could see almost as well as I did during the day. Not a "knack" I was willing to announce to just anyone, but convenient nonetheless. I'd found it to be alienating, so I hid it, a survival lesson learned as a kid.

Once I caught on to the fact that my special talent made me "odd," I pretended to fumble for a light switch or walk into an occasional chair. You'd think a kid might want to play up the superpower angle, but I kept it to myself, shoved it under a mess of other secrets I was unwilling to share, sometimes even with myself.

At first, when I was really young, I didn't know I was doing anything weird. My parents were proud when their toddler dressed in the dark and ended up with a head-to-toe matching outfit. They bragged to their friends and said I was a genius child. But eventually, when I never bothered to turn on the lights for anything, they began to get weird looks on their faces. I finally noticed that other kids couldn't do those things. And I realized that "seeing in the dark" was making Mom and Dad upset. By the time I entered grade school, I figured it was easier to pretend otherwise. I started flicking on the light switch at night, commenting on the darkness, and keeping a flashlight near my bed. Eventually, Mom and Dad stopped looking at me like I was an alien.

The thing is, I knew I was different even when no one else did. And the more I worked to be like everyone else, the bigger pain-in-the-butt teenager I became, a tidal wave that could only be stopped by something equally cataclysmic, which is exactly what happened.

Now I had come full circle. You know that saying about hindsight being twenty-twenty? Well, it had all become painfully clear last year.

How I wished I could go back and change just one thing, something so simple, something so immaterial, I'd never really miss it. I could easily have lived without going to that party, even though my friends said I'd be toast if I didn't.

But I couldn't live without her. I was trying and failing...

Last year, the worst day of my life happened. And at the end of it, I was minus a parent.

Strangely enough, the bad dreams had started a week before that, after I had watched some show about famous people researching their family history. It had been fascinating to see how these movie stars came from pretty humble beginnings. I'd started asking Mom and Dad about their families. Unfortunately, they were almost the only ones alive on both sides. Mom's only sister had died when I was a baby. Dad's only brother didn't really keep in touch, and didn't have any kids. My grandparents were gone. I asked about Uncle Ira, but they reminded me that he wasn't blood-related. He was more like a godfather to me, one I saw only occasionally. It was strange to think I was the only one left to carry on the line. I remember thinking, *Wow, hope I don't screw up the whole family tree.*

The dreams must have been a warning that my life would change forever.

After Mom...died, the dreams became worse.

Almost a year later, I still couldn't think of her without losing it. I hadn't spoken to Dad about it either. Over and over, he tried to get me to go to a doctor, but there was no way I was going to do that. He thought that if I just talked it out with someone, the nightmares would go away. He said words and feelings were just piling up inside me and found the only outlet they could—my subconscious. Sounded to me like he was the one who needed the shrink. How could talking about my mom make nightmares that had nothing to do with her go away? Yeah. Dad thought he knew what was waking me up at night. But he was so wrong.

My nightmares were like scenes from horror movies played over and over again—something chasing me, people dying, animals attacking, people turning into monsters. Yeah, messed up.

Then finally the nightmares had tapered off. I hadn't had one in at least a month, at least none that had me screaming and waking up Dad. And because of that, he cancelled my appointment. Not that I would have gone, anyway. If word got around school that I was seeing a head doctor, my already pitiful reputation would never recover from "zombie girl" (yeah, I heard what they called me behind my back).

Maybe I was fooling myself that it ever would. Maybe it didn't matter. I thought my life sucked before. But I had learned that things could always get worse, so I should be grateful for my stupid problems.

Didn't mean I couldn't complain, though. But not to my Dad, not anymore. Somehow, I was going to pull it together and turn into the adult my mom and dad had hoped for. Well, I was aiming for that, anyway.

Which brought me back to my room, and the mess in the mirror. I needed sleep. The image of a wolf chowing down on me wasn't getting me any closer to what I needed just now. Time for "old faithful."

I pulled out some scriptures Ruthie, my best friend, gave me. I had a bookmark in Genesis Four. That's where I'd stopped the last time I needed help falling asleep. Yes, I was a scripture-reading teenager. However, my motivation wasn't to get all *spiritual*—it was to get so bored, I would fall asleep. It was a tip from Ruthie—whose parents were super righteous. Ruthie called the scriptures her insomnia cure—a biblical miracle! Ha! Fortunately, it worked for me, too. I cracked the book open to Genesis Four.

And Cain talked with Abel his brother: and it came to pass, when they were in the field, that Cain rose up against Abel his brother, and slew him.

And the Lord said unto Cain, Where is Abel thy brother? And he said, I know not: Am I my brother's keeper?

And he said, What hast thou done? The voice of thy brother's blood crieth unto me from the ground.

Seriously, this Bible stuff could get pretty creepy. I wondered if I should break out my old children's book of fairy tales instead. Actually, most of them were violent, too. I turned back to Genesis.

And now art thou cursed from the earth, which hath opened her mouth to receive thy brother's blood from thy hand;

When thou tillest the ground, it shall not henceforth yield unto thee her strength; a fugitive and a vagabond shalt thou be in the earth.

Wow. But it sounded like Cain deserved it. I wondered what "cursed" meant. I yawned hugely. Almost there.

And Cain said unto the Lord, My punishment is greater than I can bear.

Behold, thou hast driven me out this day from the face of the earth; and from thy face shall I be hid; and I shall be a fugitive and a

vagabond in the earth; and it shall come to pass, that every one that findeth me shall slay me.

And the Lord said unto him, Therefore whosoever slayeth Cain, vengeance shall be taken on him sevenfold. And the Lord set a mark upon Cain, lest any finding him should kill him.

Questions twirled in my brain, and the Bible slipped from my fingers. This time the dream was not scary. It was sad.

A woman dressed in animal skins ran frantically through a grassy meadow, up to a man's body sprawled awkwardly on the ground. She fell to him, wailing, sobbing. A tall man with long, dark hair, braided down his back ran away across the meadow toward the thick copse of unusual looking trees, which seemed to be dripping, but actually had groups of long spear-like green leaves hanging from each of its long branches. Blue blossoms dangled from the tips of the leaves. Just before the man reached the trees, he cast a satisfied look behind him. The woman raised her tear-streaked gaze up and saw it. Her features pinched as she pointed toward him, her long, elegant arm seeming to pierce him. Fear struck the man's face and he made one final leap into the safety of the trees just as a burst of heat shot past him hitting the blue-belled tree. The woman screamed in anguish toward the purple sky, revenge still burning in her eyes. She pulled the slain man into her lap, whispering, "My love."

I awoke with tears on my face. The first day of school was officially here. Not a great start.

2

Checklist

I DRIED OFF AFTER an extra long shower and went about my morning preparations. Repeating the mantra that Ruthie made me promise to say every morning since she came back from vacation. Yeah, she probably got it from a fortune cookie, but whatever.

"Whatever the mind conceives and believes, it achieves."

Then I was supposed to imagine the way I wanted my day to go. I closed my eyes tightly and tried to see myself as I wanted to be today.

I got nothing. Honestly, I couldn't imagine what today was going to be like, at least in a positive way. So I thought about the good parts of my life.

Right now, the best thing I had going were my grades. School was easy for me, always had been, and since I didn't goof off in class (unlike my best friend), the teachers liked me. Thank goodness, because after my mom died, I dropped out of sports, clubs, and my social life. The teachers must have felt sorry for me, because I pulled better grades than I deserved. However, that scholarship to Stanford was out of the question now.

Sophomore year was like running through water, and I was exhausted at the end of each day. I think I slept most of it. I got through the worst with the help of my best friend. Everyone else bailed on me, which was probably fair because I bailed on them first when I dropped out of everything, even the conversations.

"Stop that, girlfriend!" I channeled Ruthie and smiled, thinking I got her tone of voice right. I had to think positively.

With my towel wrapped around me, I headed to my room to dress. I ran my hand over the framed picture on my dresser. Mom and I were laughing so hard we were holding each other up. I couldn't remember why we were laughing exactly, just that it was one of those silly giggle episodes that got out of control. I needed some of that silliness now.

A year ago, you couldn't get me to think too deeply about anything. Now I thought too much. It was driving me crazy. *Yeah, I know I should see a shrink, but it's so not going to happen.*

How utterly surreal to look at that picture and know that vibrant person was dead. I never thought much about death before the accident. I mean, who does, right? I saw death all the time, on TV, in the news, even joked about it. Yet nothing prepared you for the real thing. Would it have been easier if I had just been told she was dead? Perhaps. However, witnessing a death is much more life changing than I thought it would be. Alive one second and so not the next—at least I think so. It was still very hazy in my mind. One more reason Dad wanted me to "talk" to someone. He thought I was blocking out the memory, but really I just didn't remember much of it. I do remember seeing the impact of the car as it ran over Mom. I remember seeing her dead. I'll never forget that horror. And I couldn't let go of the feeling that it was my fault, like I had killed her.

Anyway, I thought I was stronger. You know, the whole lecture about "she'll always be with you," "she would want you to be happy," "you aren't the only one hurting." Yeah, surprise, surprise. Those sentiments don't really make you feel better. I was only sixteen, and the person who helped me get to that pivotal age wouldn't be there to help me through the rest, which would undoubtedly be way more difficult.

I had been a total mess last year.

The school year had almost come to an end before I noticed a change. It was like thawing out after swimming in the freezing Pacific Ocean. Feeling began returning to my lifeless heart and spread to the tips of my fingers and toes—like a transfusion of life, but I don't remember getting hooked up to anything. I'm not sure what triggered it—it just happened. I didn't realize how far I had regressed until I actually felt something again. No, that's not the best description. It was like not using a muscle for such a long time, it atrophied, forgot how to work. That's how my life was, atrophied. Yes, that's a better way to explain it. So I resolved to work harder and made a list of things to change about myself.

I ran my finger over my mom's face in the picture frame, whispering, "I'm trying really hard, Mom."

Toward the end of summer, I'd recommitted myself to life. I decided it was time to make a comeback, painful though it might be—which was why I couldn't look like crap on the first day of school.

Staring into my mirrored closet doors, I felt grateful once again to Uncle Ira for getting me the job at the rec center this summer. I still hadn't thanked him because he'd been out of touch most of the break. He did that a lot. We went sometimes months without a word or way to contact him. I didn't mind so much because when he was around, he kind of spooked me. I often caught him watching me, like he was waiting for me to do something. What? I didn't know. But sometimes I wondered if he knew some of my secrets. Why would I think that? I don't know. It was just a feeling. So I didn't mind that he wasn't around all that much.

However, he had been there for me several times over the worst of the past year—that I could remember. Or at least Dad said so. Uncle Ira seemed to really care, so I pushed aside my own odd impressions of him. And I wanted him to see how much better I was, thanks to the job he found me.

I loved working with kids' basketball and lifeguarding. Who knew I would? I'd been reluctant to do it, sure it would end in epic failure and kids scarred for life, but eventually I agreed to try it out.

That I was good at it surprised me as much as my dad. It had helped me get back in shape, physically and emotionally, plus I'd earned a great tan.

So check "pasty white skin" off my list of things to fix.

And although they say girls don't grow much in high school, I was the exception. I had gone from "sturdy-looking" to long and curvy. Total freaking miracle, or so my best friend would say. My lack of appetite the year before (or maybe the lack of mom's cooking) had a lot to do with it, I'm sure.

Check "nondescript body" off the list.

None of my clothes fit me by the end of summer. Let's just say school shopping was a blast this year. Dad gulped at the receipt each time he left a store. I tried to rationalize that we were simply making up for not buying new clothes for so long. But it didn't seem to help him fork over the money any easier. The only thing that did help was the smile I wore.

Yes, check "catatonic" off the list.

Dad had been so happy about a stupid smile that I began to realize for the first time how worried about me he had been.

When I started going places again (*check "introvert" off the list*), he practically flipped cartwheels. Then he began to notice the differences in me. I had turned that corner from awkward teen to adult over the summer (better late than never). He suddenly changed his tune and started asking me a million questions every time I left the house. He worried needlessly. I didn't do much besides work because my best friend was gone for the summer, and the rest of my friends had given up on me last year when I stopped responding to them. I'd made a few friends at the rec center, but the most we did together was have lunch or play basketball. Besides, I was content with less. For now at least. I was easing into this new "me."

Now Ruthie was back. We had hung out every day for the last week, trying to catch up, and we were looking forward to our junior year.

Check off "no friends."

I began to have hope for more. I gave myself one last inspection in the mirror. "It's now or never," I whispered to my reflection. Then I headed out.

3

Cujo

By the time I got downstairs, Dad had my lunch packed and a box of cereal on the table. You'd think I could make my own lunch by now.

"Hey, Sunshine!" Dad said, looking up from his newspaper and peering over the rims of his glasses.

I was certainly not feeling sunny. First-day-of-school butterflies were swarming in my stomach. I was excited and terrified at the same time. No. Blustery or scattered thunderstorms seemed more appropriate.

"How'd you sleep?"

"Great," I lied, raising my voice an octave. Dad lowered his newspaper and I saw the ugly scratch along his face. The butterflies in my stomach stopped flying and got sick. What kind of freak attacks her dad?

"Aw, Dad! I'm sorry about your face!" I joined him at the table and poured some cereal into the empty bowl set out for me.

"What, this ol' thing?" He ran his finger down the scratch. "The guys at work are gonna love it! I'll tell them I was in a bar fight. Yeah, that sounds good."

"Hate to break it to you, but don't guys give each other black eyes and broken noses? Besides, you don't drink. That scratch looks more like you were girl fighting..."

Dad raised his eyebrows. "You're right!" He leaned forward. "Go ahead. Punch me in the eye. Make it look good." I giggled. The butterflies calmed. When I was younger, Dad would wrestle with me in the living room, and I always tried to get him in the eye, not that I ever got close. We got into trouble with Mom a lot.

"Hey! You know the rules: no fighting in the house..." I trailed off—that's exactly what Mom would have said. Dad froze, just for a second, and I saw the shadows in his eyes. He tried to hide it by tilting away from me, but I saw them.

He cleared his throat and said, "Yeah, yeah... Uh, I probably don't need to go into the office for a couple of days anyway. I'm supposed to be semi-retired, for Pete's sake. I'll just remind them again. No worries. It will be gone soon enough." I was doubtful. He started folding the newspaper.

"Okay. You planning to hide out here until then?" I tried to patch up my blunder, but it wasn't working. I couldn't believe I said that. He'd been trying to get me to talk about Mom forever, but the first time I even remotely allude to her in almost a year—well, even he wasn't ready. The walls were starting to close in on me, and my breathing picked up.

I had to get out of there before he noticed. As if planned, a car honked outside.

"Yeah, um, I gotta go..."

Dad followed me to the door, grabbing my lunch bag on the way.

"No time for breakfast, I guess. Good thing I packed a little extra in your lunch." He dropped the sack into my empty backpack, and leaned over to kiss my cheek. Part of me felt guilty for running off.

"Thanks, Dad." I gave him a one-armed squeeze and kissed him back. I hoped the scratch would go away fast, not just for him, but for me, too. I ran my finger down the length of the pink line. The morning light chose that moment to peek in, and it lit up his skin. I blinked and looked at his scar again. It already seemed to be fading. I laughed silently at my silliness, but it made me feel a little better. I guess you saw what you wanted to see.

"Have a good day, Dad."

"You, too, honey. And good luck. Can't wait to hear how it goes." He knew how nervous I was for this day, how much I had to make up for my dismal existence last year.

As I swung open the door, the crisp morning air sent a chill through me and I shivered. I debated on grabbing a jacket, but didn't want to delay my exit. The school classrooms were always mega hot, anyway.

Finally I was out the door. I took a long, deep, cleansing breath like they taught in the yoga classes at the rec center, minus the sweeping hands, and headed down the walkway. Ruthie was waiting in her red Mini Cooper convertible, top down, a superstar smile splitting her face. She was one of the few juniors who could drive her friends around. Being held back a year in first grade landed her in my class, which is where our friendship had started. She had earned her license her sophomore year, unlike the rest of the class. Around here, you have to drive a year before you can drive underage passengers. This was the first time she could drive me to school, and we were both ecstatic.

Ruthie's parents were so proud of her for passing all her driving tests the first time through, they bought her a new car last year. Where's the justice? As jealous as I was, I was grateful to have a friend with wheels any time I needed them. I threw my backpack over the seat and climbed in. Ruthie grabbed me in a hug.

"I still can't believe the new you! Where do you have my best friend stashed, you body-snatching alien!" she screamed.

I'd missed her enthusiasm. Ruthie had been gone most of the summer at church camps, family reunions, and her grandma's farm up in Idaho. She kept checking me out—from anyone else, it would be creepy. I just rolled my eyes at her as she continued.

"I give you one week before you have a boyfriend. That's about right. You look fine!" She drew out the word fine like the last note in a song, emphasizing it with her hands. I couldn't care less about a boyfriend. I'd never really been boy crazy like Ruthie; however, it didn't prevent me from enjoying all the gossip she threw my way. High school traditions meant a lot to her, and a boyfriend was definitely on her list of high school expectations. Last year was a wash, but I could see that this year she was going to make me a personal project. My goal, however, was to reach normal status, and anything beyond that was icing on the cake—I just hoped she didn't get too disappointed with me.

"Ruthie, you better watch the road," I sputtered, grasping the door handle as the car squealed onto the road. I was still getting used to Ruthie's driving.

"And," I continued, "don't start setting me up. I don't want a boyfriend. Let's just see if anyone even notices me—in a non-zombie kind of way. Maybe I could start with having a friend who is a boy."

"Would you stop with that zombie thing? No one will remember last year. That's the beauty of high school, you get to reboot your rep every year."

"If you say so. Besides, you're the one who won't be single long." She looked better than ever. "I'm thinking the farm life really agrees with you."

Her dark brown hair had a burgundy wash to it, making the overall color look very high end. It hung in waves just past her shoulders. Hazel eyes were outlined expertly with liner and mascara. Ruthie had filled out nicely way back in middle school. So not fair to the rest of the curve-challenged girls, me included. But she was a year older, and I guess you could say that was the best advantage of being held back a grade—she was ahead in the body department. She would have had a hundred dates by now, except her parents wouldn't let her date until she turned seventeen. She coped with secret boyfriends mostly during school hours or activities. I did my best-friend duty, helping her sneak now and then. It got a little dicey a few times, but for the most part, her family had managed to keep her "sweet and pure" as Ruthie joked. Then her long-awaited birthday had finally come at the end of last school year, just before her family dragged her off on one trip after another. I had a feeling they did that on purpose, and I knew she wanted to make up for lost time.

"You said it, sister! Can I just say farm boys are sexy!"

"What? You never told me about a farm boy!" She was holding out on me. We'd been keeping in touch off and on all summer by phone. You'd think she would have mentioned that.

"I was saving it for today. Besides, it was just one kiss." Her lips twisted up at one corner and down the other, a specialty of hers when she didn't get her way. "The day before I came home. But it was awesome, you know? Best goodbye I ever had."

I wouldn't know. Not that I was saving my first kiss for anyone special, but no kisses had come my way, at least none that I wanted. Playground kisses didn't count. And since then, my options had been pretty slim. The loser squad that hung out smoking at the edge of campus always seemed interested, but they also seemed into any girl who walked by. Can I just say "Gross!" Seriously, kissing a cigarette mouth made me want to yak.

"Actually, no, I wouldn't know." I gave her a wry smile.

"Yeah, right. Sorry, I forgot—sh...shank steak!" Ruthie veered sharply to the right and hit the brakes. As a vegetarian who was trying to quit swearing, she had begun substituting cusswords with different meat entrées.

"Did you see that? There it is!" Ruthie pointed to the side of the road, where the trees began.

I couldn't believe it! It was the wolf in my dreams, dark brown with light-colored markings around its face and underbelly. The fur looked incredibly thick, even from this distance. And the wolf seemed to glance back at us before it faded into the tall bushes next to the road. We were on an old road that was considered "deep woods" until about ten years ago when several new housing developments went in, my parents' for one. A forest conservation group had stepped in before all the houses were finished, and nothing new had been built in our neighborhood since then. We often saw wildlife along the road, but this was something new.

"Tru, that was a freakin' big dog! I've never seen anything like it. And damn—I mean, dang, if I didn't see a lot of animals this summer! That must be a cross between a Great Dane and a German shepherd, you think? That thing needs its own corral!" At my silence, Ruthie looked at me.

"Hey, are you okay? Did you bump your head or something? Sorry I stopped so fast."

My vocal cords finally remembered how to work. "No, I'm fine." I cleared my throat. "You just really scared me for a second. How'd you ever get a license?" I joked hollowly, the image of the wolf still flashing through my head.

"Ha! Ha! I probably saved your life *and* ol' Cujo's back there." She swept her hair over her shoulder and pulled back onto the road, carefully checking her mirrors. A couple summers ago, Ruthie and I decided to become horror movie experts, starting with the old classics like the killer dog movie *Cujo* and the ghost movie *Lady in White*, ending with the *Scream* series. She'd slept with the lights on for at least two months; I just didn't sleep.

"You mean wolf," I said.

"What? Wolf? No way. We don't have wolves around here, silly. Just coyotes. And maybe wild dogs."

"When did you become a wildlife expert?" I laughed. "Yeah, I'm probably wrong. It's just so weird."

"Tell me about it! I wonder what it means, you know, first day of school and all. It must be a sign or something."

Ruthie was always trying to find a special meaning in every event that happened in her life. She also liked to sneak in a horoscope reading when she could, although she always insisted she didn't really believe in them. Her veggie persona had been born when she entered high school. The newly defined Ruthie seemed to give her a place in the crazy high school factory of "un-originals." I could understand, I guess.

So what are the odds that I would dream about a wolf (aka very large dog) the night before one crossed my path, literally? Maybe Ruthie was on to something. Maybe if I figured out some of these dreams, I would stop having the dumb nightmares.

"What would you say if told you I dreamed about a wolf last night?"

"No sh...stuffed veal, girl! You better spill right now!"

Not sure if I should have mentioned my crazy dreams, I made it short and sweet.

"Oh, I don't know. I'm in this smoky forest and this wolf howls and runs up to me and, you know, chomps me. That's when I wake up. Silly, huh?" I'd left out the screaming and waking up Dad part.

"That is *supa-freaky*! It's a sign for sure. Something out there is trying to talk to you. New you, new grade. You feel overwhelmed. And maybe you, like, physically manifested your fears into a large dog running across the road. Whoa! You have some kind of psychic power, girl! That's awesome!"

Maybe, but it was more like I had some *psycho* power. No small stretch for me to believe that one. Who needs a shrink when you have a best friend...

4

BROWN EYES

BY THE TIME RUTHIE and I rolled into the school parking lot, we were back to discussing the most important things in a teenage girl's life—clothes and boys. Just like old times.

"You have to show me where you got those jeans! The pockets rock!" Ruthie gushed. "Okay, how's the makeup?" She pursed her lips and gave me her most seductive look. I rolled my eyes.

"Are you kidding? You look perfect, as usual. You remind me of Jennifer on *Court of Palms*," I assured her. *Court of Palms* was Ruthie's favorite teen soap, and she considered Jennifer the hottest girl on the show. I only watched it when we were hanging out.

Ruthie commentated each episode with paparazzi-like detail. A spontaneous giggle bubbled up inside me at the memory, but it was pierced with a happy cry at the fond memories and sudden gratitude that I had my best friend back.

She stared at me, wide-eyed, moisture welling up in them. "Oh, Tru!" She started fanning herself. "You've been watching our show!"

I gave her a trembling grin. "Of course! I had to catch up on all that soap smut before you got home so we could be ready for the new season, right?" To Ruthie, this was one of the best ways for me to show I was 100 percent back to BFF status.

"Oh, good gravy, girl! You're gonna wreck my mascara!" She gave me a smile, fanning her watery eyes with her hands.

"But...like..." I amended with my best valley girl accent, "Don't let it all out at once. You better, like, put on your Prada glasses."

With a wink, she played along. "You are so right! They can't handle all of me yet." She pulled out her black Prada glasses, which looked great with her purple belted tunic and skinny jeans. A long gold chain hung down to her stomach, which somehow emphasized her ample chest—a purposeful move on her part, I was sure. Large gold hoops swung from her ears. She finished her outfit with black mid-high sandals, giving her more height than she normally had.

My ensemble was mild in comparison. The topaz jewels on my back pockets were my only adornment. The jeans were dark denim. The yellow stitching stood out, emphasizing the back pockets and elongating my legs, which ended in gold Converses. *Yes, gold. How awesome is that?* My white T-shirt had a gold and brown owl on the front—profile only, thank goodness, because two owl eyes on my chest was asking for the wrong kind of attention. The T-shirt fit snugly in all the right places. My hair hung in waves down my back, my "golden lava look," according to Ruthie. While Ruthie went all out on the makeup, I stuck to mascara and lip gloss. Ruthie disliked my makeup-less style, but she rarely pressured me to wear more since our makeovers at the mall. She had looked chic and fashionable while I had resembled a Vegas street walker. I stuck to neutrals after that.

Even though I knew I looked better than I ever had at this school, I couldn't bring myself to open the car door. Facing everyone after being such a loser last year was starting to bring on a minor panic attack. Unfortunately, I knew what one was because I'd had one in front of everyone—my worst school moment ever. Ruthie noticed my dilemma. She reached over and hugged me.

"Tru, you seriously have nothing to worry about. Your new hotness will cancel out last year like it never happened. Trust me!"

More thankful than I could say, I hugged her back.

"Let's do this," I said, and reached for the car handle.

"Who is that?!" exclaimed Ruthie.

I looked out the windshield. Walking through the parking lot in front of us was, well, a really hot guy who looked familiar. And beside him was the most gracefully beautiful girl I had ever seen.

"Holy tri-tip! That's Isaac and Phoebe Efoti!" Ruthie's jaw hung open. So did mine.

"No way! They look like they grew a whole foot since I last saw them. And wow!" I lost my train of thought. "Wow," I repeated. Had I been so out of it that I hadn't noticed how much everyone around me had changed? No, I was sure they had looked very different at the end of the previous school year.

I remembered Isaac as cute in a short and adorable kind of way. No one was going to describe him like a teddy bear this year. I had gone to school with him last year, but I hadn't gotten to know him very well. Walking across my vision, he looked like the kind of guy you asked for help when you needed to move a piano—upstairs, three stories. He towered over the other students, and his neck and shoulders were lumberjack thick. I remembered he was some beach bum kind of boy. I could easily see him jogging down a beach with a surfboard. I kind of liked envisioning him running down the shore.

His sister, Phoebe, glided alongside him. She looked like a Hawaiian princess, or that actress turned princess, Grace somebody, only Polynesian. While Isaac sported curly dark hair, with sun-bleached ends, Phoebe's hair was smooth and straight, like ebony fabric. They totally didn't look like twins, but they did look related.

"Man!" whispered Ruthie. "They must feel like giants next to their mom. She's from Taiwan, I think, and I never thought the twins would get tall, let alone awesome tall. Double dang! Looks like they're going with the Tongan DNA."

"Yeah," I said. Now I remembered what I knew about their parents. Their dad, a Pacific Islander, was more of an average-sized guy, definitely under six feet. But even so, he looked like the Incredible Hulk next to their mom.

"Did you know that Isaac had a crush on you last year?" asked Ruthie.

"Really?" I was surprised. "You never told me."

"Well, you would have noticed yourself if you weren't...well, you know," she finished lamely.

She was referring to my dark phase, the year I wanted to forget. But even though I didn't remember the details, I was constantly reminded of the consequences. It was going to haunt me forever. Luckily, Ruthie hadn't totally bailed on our friendship like all my other friends. She'd been loyal the whole time, hanging out with me even when I was dead boring. I hadn't had the energy to invest on other friends, and one by one, they had dropped away. I had been an emotional dark hole. So it was no surprise, really, that I never noticed someone taking an interest in me. Besides, as I recalled, I was pretty dweeby-looking my first two years of high school—and I had the yearbook pictures to prove it. Who would have thought anyone like Isaac would be interested?

"Oh yeah, you hung out with them a lot last year, right?" I sidestepped the delicate subject of mental absence last year.

Ruthie gave me a considering look.

"Well, you'll always be my best friend, Tru, but I needed to re-energize with a few others last year, because, well...you just needed some space."

"Ruthie—"

"No, it's totally okay!" she consoled me. "I probably would have lost it, too. But, look." She squeezed my hand. "You're back. You were coming back before I left for the summer. It really sucked that my parents made me leave." She grimaced, but then turned back to look through her windshield. "Hey, it's a new year and for freakin' fried chicken! Isaac Efoti is a hottie! Did you see him?"

I laughed. She pronounced Isaac's last name wrong to make it rhyme with "hottie." It was going to hang around my brain like the chorus to a good song. But that was so Ruthie.

"You go, girl!" I said. "I may have to amend your boyfriend projection. Who needs a week?" Laughing, we hurried out of the car to cut a path toward the twins.

"Hey, Phoebe! Isaac!" yelled Ruthie. They looked like they were about to step around the first building when they heard her.

Phoebe was the first to react. She swung back and screamed, "Ruthie!" When we caught up, they grabbed each other for a hug. That left me looking at Mr. Hottie Efoti.

He must have been six and a half feet, towering over my not-so-short 5'9" stature. And he looked like he just stepped off the pages of *Island Beach Babes.* His full Polynesian lips widened when he saw me, and his white teeth stood out on his tan, sculpted face. His big brown eyes twinkled under his long, curly eyelashes. *Wow*, I thought again. When I got to his eyes, I noticed him checking me out, too. I felt my face go red.

"Hey, Parker," he greeted in a deep, husky voice. I was ga-ga enough to think that him calling me by my last name was cute.

"Isaac. So...how was the beach this summer?"

"A little crowded for me, but that didn't stop me from catchin' some sick waves!" He smiled widely, and his teeth actually looked bleached next to his tanned skin. *He should do dental commercials,* I thought. *Man! What were we talking about?* I had totally lost the train of our conversation, and I felt my face warm in embarrassment. I quickly found the sidewalk to be very interesting.

Ruthie saved me by hauling herself at Isaac, who despite the full force of her body blow did not move an inch. He just swept her up into a hug. I totally felt out of the loop now. How did I miss this last year?

Ruthie held both of them under her arms—well, at least she tried. Instead, she ended up with her arms more around their waists. A little part of me was jealous. Maybe a large part.

Ruthie said, "Man, I missed you guys this summer!"

"Me too!" said Phoebe. "But don't feel bad about taking off. We were hardly here. We had a lot of, uh, family stuff going on." She exchanged a look with Isaac before turning to me.

"How...was...your...summer...Tru?" She talked slowly, and overemphasized her words like she was speaking to a three-year-old.

If I was pink before, I was cherry red now.

"Geez, Phoebe, she's not an idiot!" Isaac reprimanded. Ruthie looked a little surprised. "Can't you see her summer was very good to her?" His eyes locked onto mine like radar, and I couldn't look away. He began to sing, low and magnetically. I could almost see waves in the air pulling me toward him.

His big voice was raspy like a country singer, but the song was some old band boy tune that I knew but couldn't place because the way he sang it was much more intimate. I felt like we were alone, just the two of us, and that I was the center of his world—

"Please! The Jonas Brothers? Really?!" Phoebe interrupted my drooling, rolling her eyes. I blinked. Ruthie and I were suddenly very close to him. I couldn't decide if I should melt into a pool of embarrassment or run for the hills. I settled for picking my jaw off the ground and dipping my head to allow my hair to cover my awkwardness. *What just happened?* I wondered. Those were the corniest lyrics ever, but somehow so amazing.

I peeked over at Phoebe. She was reassessing me. I just wanted to sink into the ground—she had caught me drooling over her brother! Talk about awkward. I noticed her arm on Isaac's. I didn't remember seeing her move. Was I losing it? I shook my head as if to clear it.

Ruthie roared with laughter. "Oh my gosh, Isaac!" she sputtered, fanning herself. "You should try out for *Idol!*" I felt a little better seeing Ruthie just as breathless as I. But still. Way awkward!

How could he do that? I puzzled. He didn't show an eensie bit of embarrassment after breaking into song—in public, no less. Not that he should feel self-conscious. His voice was a sexy, deep baritone and the words had sizzled me down to my bones. Obviously, since Ruthie and I had almost jumped him.

Phoebe smacked Isaac hard in the stomach.

"Don't do that!" she said, almost angrily.

"Ow!" He looked a little chagrinned. It was actually funny to see him cowering from his smaller sister.

"Seriously, you are such a dog!" laughed Phoebe. Isaac just smiled, clearly proud of himself. His smug look annoyed me.

I noticed Ruthie fluttering her long eyelashes spastically, apparently ready to start an Isaac fan club.

"So, you're back in the real world, now, are you?" Phoebe asked, appraising me again.

Ruthie finally pulled her gaze from Isaac and said, "Yes! Yes! Yes!" before cheerfully throwing her arm around me. "It's awesome!"

The warning bell rang. Isaac was smiling widely, clearly aware of his effect on us. I hated that he made me feel like a slow, gawky girl. And there was something that didn't feel right about it, anyway. Ruthie grabbed my arm and started pulling. I narrowed my eyes at him and let her drag me away.

"We'll catch up with you guys at lunch if we don't have any classes with you before then. Let's compare schedules!"

She started running, and I took off with her, my backpack slapping against my back in our rush. We both had Mr. Pham's Algebra II class first period.

Mr. Pham was writing on the board as we hurried in just as the bell rang, trying to be nonchalant about our lateness. We found two seats next to each other on the far side and slid into them just as he put down his marker.

Ruthie pulled out her binder and scribbled on a piece of paper. She passed it to me.

I read her hasty scribbles. *What the ~~hell~~ ham hocks was that all about?* I looked up at her and just shrugged. She snagged back the note, ran her pencil across it, and slipped it back to me. *He still likes you!*

I wasn't one for getting in trouble in class and didn't want to risk the teacher's wrath the first day by passing notes. So I just mouthed "later" to her, slipped the note into my binder, and turned my attention to the teacher. Besides, my reaction to Isaac bothered me. That had just been weird.

5

Blue Eyes

RUTHIE AND I DIDN'T have any classes together for the rest of the day. We had already compared our schedules over the weekend. I knew most of the kids in my classes, but they didn't seem to recognize me. The guys looked me over with interest, the girls with curiosity, at least until my name was called for attendance. Then people really looked at me. They stared and whispered. Awkward. My attempt at "normal" didn't seem to be working out this year. With each ensuing class, I shrank deeper and deeper into my seat, hoping to get the day over as fast as possible. I practically ran from my Physics class. I headed out the door and planned to keep walking until I walked through my front door, but something turned me toward the quad, where everyone hung out for lunch. It made me pause enough to rethink my situation.

Dad would probably make me see the shrink if I skipped school today. With a resigned sigh, I changed my mind and decided to stake out the usual table Ruthie and I liked, near a large maple tree. I was early and the tables were still unoccupied, so I thought I could "lose it" for a second without anyone noticing. I slammed down on the bench and leaned over onto the table.

"Freakin' stupid school!" I exclaimed into my arms.

"Wow. And the day's only half over," said a low voice.

There was that feeling again, like a warm current of air on a cold day. Now I knew exactly where it was coming from. I sat up straight and glared toward the tree trunk. Sure enough, someone was lounging at its base, backpack next to him. He crunched into an apple. Great. A witness to my latest meltdown. Thank goodness I hadn't started crying. The guy stood up, out of the shade, and took two strides to my table, sitting down next to me with his body pointing away from the table, elbows on the table behind him.

Okay. As bugged as I was that he had eavesdropped on my misery, there was no stopping the sudden thumping of my heart as I took inventory; I seemed helpless to do anything else at that moment.

Dark chestnut hair and blue eyes, *dark* blue eyes. His hair was thick and just long enough to curl at the ends, flipping up near the part on the side of his head. His straight nose, only marred by the slightest bump, ended at a masculine point over—can I just say—the most perfect mouth, the type of mouth you see on Greek statues. A wave of familiarity swept over me. Had we met before? Oh man, it was probably last year when I was so out of it.

"Sorry if I scared you." He was starting to look concerned. Not him, too, I thought angrily.

"Oh, yeah. No—no, you...uh...just surprised me, that's all," I stuttered. He reciprocated with a deep chuckle and held out his hand.

"Zander. You?"

I offered my hand automatically. As our palms touched, a warm, humming sensation enveloped my arm. It reminded me how I felt when petting a purring cat. He looked just as surprised as I did. We released our hands quickly.

"Whoa. Must be some kind of static shock or something. Sorry. I'm Tru. Are you new here?" He stared at me more intently than before, like he was trying to decide whether or not to reply. *Could my day get any weirder?* I wondered. Homeschooling was starting to sound good.

I was fairly sure I'd never seen him before. He looked like a senior, with his shadowy jaw. Yes, he shaved, and without any nicks like half the population around here. His neck was corded with muscle, although he didn't look steroid-bulky, more athletic and healthy.

He finally seemed to come to a decision. "Yeah. Moved here at the end of summer."

"Really? Senior?"

"I wish. My parents pulled me out of school last year so much, I have to retake my classes." He leaned closer. "So I'm probably the oldest junior here."

"Actually—" I started to say.

Just then, Ruthie called out, "Hey, you got here fast!" She was followed by Isaac and Phoebe. They spread out around the circular table and looked questioningly at Zander.

"Oh, hi guys. Yeah, my, uh, class got out a little early." Like I was going to tell them I ran out of class to cry like a baby. I shot Zander a surreptitious glance, hoping he wouldn't mention my little table tantrum. He raised an eyebrow at me, but said nothing.

I gestured toward my new acquaintance. "This is Zander. He's new this year." Zander gave Phoebe and Isaac that assessing look he had given me. Isaac seemed to dislike him on sight. Phoebe gave him the tilted-head half-smile look, aka the "come hither" look. So obvious. But I couldn't blame her. And I wouldn't blame him for falling for it—she was just as beautiful as he was.

"Cool! We need some fresh blood here at our table," said Ruthie, drinking in every inch of him. I could almost read her mind. She was in heaven. Two gorgeous guys at our lunch table. We'd really stepped up in the world. Ruthie was going to have to swat away the girls who would soon be flocking our way.

Here we go, I thought as a giggling squad of girls sashayed past our table, their eyes trying to catch those of both Isaac and Zander, who were still squaring off. I was surprised to see two old friends from my old basketball team, but they totally ignored me. I had to admit it hurt a little, but I reminded myself that I probably did the same thing to them last year.

Then the moment passed, and after one of those guy nods, Isaac ignored Zander and turned his big brown eyes on me. "So how are your classes so far? Did you get Mrs. Tisdale for English?"

Having his total focus on me made me feel conspicuous. He ignored everyone else, and there was just so much of him. It reminded me of earlier when he sang to me, and remembering my reaction made my cheeks heat up again, especially since Zander was watching with a slight scowl on his face. Why did this feel so awkward? Any girl would be into Isaac, right? Why did I feel guilty suddenly?

I decided to ignore the first question—I had nothing good to say about my classes so far, and I didn't want to complain, yet. I would unload it all on Ruthie later.

"No, I've got Mr. Mac." That's what we called him; his name was actually Macintosh. He was Scottish, with the cool accent and everything. I loved to hear him read out loud. And he happened to be pretty good-looking, for a teacher. Girls were known to stare at him throughout the entire class, especially when he read Shakespeare. He gave off an Ewan McGregor vibe with the whole accent and good looks thing. He got pretty frustrated sometimes because he had to repeat himself all the time. Personally, I thought it was entertaining.

"No kidding," Zander piped in. "I've got him too, seventh period." He did seem like a nice guy. Most guys would have run the other way from a girl on the verge of a breakdown.

"Oh, cool," I said, smiling. Perhaps if he never found out how weird I was last year, he'd actually keep talking to me.

"Let me see your schedule, Tru. Maybe we have something together, too." Isaac scooted closer, tipping the table as he adjusted his weight, causing Ruthie to squeal.

Zander frowned, then stood up. "Gotta run. I'm supposed to meet with my counselor about some paperwork. I'll see you in English, Tru."

"Sure. See you then." I watched him as he stepped back to the tree to snag his backpack. He hesitated there, turning back to us, like he was rethinking his actions. But with a tightening of his jaw, he twisted away and loped off across the pod. I felt a strange desire to follow him. My heart squeezed and I had to make myself breathe slowly. I was so messed up!

All three of us girls watched him, enjoying the view.

"Nice..." drawled Phoebe. My heart tightened uncomfortably at their slack jaws. Then I saw Phoebe glance quickly over at Isaac, who was scowling. She rolled her eyes.

"Okay, let's all get our schedules out and compare," suggested Phoebe.

As it turned out, I had a class with each of them. First period with Ruthie for Algebra II, fifth period with Isaac for drama, and sixth period with Phoebe for PE. Originally, I had been peeved to be stuck in drama, which was way out of my comfort zone, but knowing Isaac would be there with me took away some of the sting. At least I'd know someone who would talk to me in all of my afternoon classes. And maybe I could figure out what bothered me about him. Ruthie and Isaac had two classes together already, but only World Civilization with Phoebe.

By the time lunch was over, several guys had stopped by to chat with Phoebe, and just as many girls had hit on Isaac. I wasn't surprised, but it was getting old really fast. Ruthie also caught up with some old acquaintances. Fortunately, Isaac kept me from feeling like a total pariah. I couldn't help but give him points for that.

Ruthie and I were dumping our trash when Val Johnson, Ruthie's first ever boyfriend back in middle school, stopped by to ask her about her classes. Despite my personal prediction that he would turn into a class nerd (which I'd told Ruthie to console her after they broke up in eighth grade), he'd become a school jock, and turned out pretty smokin' hot himself. Unfortunately, it came with a typical jock personality. Ruthie didn't seem to mind, though. She gave me the "I'll catch up with you later" look. So I waved goodbye and took off to my locker to get my stuff for drama.

"Hey, don't forget me!" called Isaac.

I'd already forgotten we had the next class together. To be honest, I was wondering about Zander and his deep blue eyes. Isaac was being really nice to me, and there I was zoning off about another boy.

"Sorry. I have to stop by my locker first."

"No worries. I'll walk with you!"

"Thanks," I said, smiling up at him. How shallow was I to feel this awesome about walking to class with a guy who looked like a beach model?

6

HORMONES

AS OUR DRAMA TEACHER went over the classroom rules, I had to keep my hand over my mouth so that I didn't burst out giggling. Isaac mimicked the teacher with amazing accuracy. If he didn't go anywhere with his singing, he definitely had a career in acting. But apparently, the rest of the class wasn't as talented. Their reactions eventually tipped off the teacher.

"Mr. Efoti, I'm glad to see that you are such a natural entertainer." Mr. Romano peered at us, a small smile on his lips. "Perhaps you can put that charm to good use and begin our game of charades."

Thankfully, Mr. Romano wasn't angry and seemed to know how to handle Isaac's playfulness. The rest of the period showed us who the real hams were in the class. I was *not* one of them, and thankfully the bell rang before my turn arrived.

As I started to rise, Isaac, who was already standing, blocked me by crouching down beside my desk. His face was so close to mine I could see every eyelash surrounding his golden brown eyes. He smelled woodsy and minty.

"Tru, uh, I just wanted to say that I'm glad you're back to normal this year."

I felt my face heat up, remembering last year. Isaac quickly backpedaled.

"I know it was awful and everything, about your mom, but I'm just glad to see you smiling again."

I thought he was very sweet to say so, but I really did *not* want to talk about my mom or my horrible existence last year. So I pasted on a smile and said, "Life sucks sometimes, but eventually you move on."

That's what my dad said to me, and even though I did not feel like I was *over it*, I agreed that I had to move on. One corner of Isaac's mouth turned up, and he grabbed my hand and squeezed.

"I've gotta get over to Mr. Dao's class," he said. It was on the other side of campus. "But I'll see you after school!"

I shook my head with bemusement as I watched him stride away. Students and teachers alike moved out of his way, his sheer size bringing out their sense of self-preservation. Top that off with his soft brown skin, sun-kissed hair, and rippling muscles—well, I was surprised he didn't have a crowd of groupies pursuing him yet. But it was just the first day of school, and I knew it was only a matter of time.

My thoughts strayed to Zander as I headed to my next class. Although he wasn't the hulking hotness that Isaac was, he was sure to attract his own "whore horde," which is what Ruthie called the girl packs who hung out at guys' lockers and followed them everywhere.

PE wasn't as bad as I thought it would be. Phoebe sat beside me on the gym bleachers as we listened to the teacher make her first-day-of-class speech, followed by locker assignments. Although we weren't friends, she didn't treat me as if I were a plague victim like the other kids did. I dared to think we could even be friends.

Evidently, if Phoebe Efoti could stand sitting by me, then I must not be too bad. Most of the other girls eyed Phoebe warily, almost like they were scared of her. Perhaps that's why she sat with me. We both seemed to be outsiders. I could see why Phoebe put them off. She was almost too confident and had little patience for idiots, demonstrated by the number of times she laughed at the questions. Admittedly, they were lame, but she certainly wasn't winning any friends by pointing that out.

We were finally left to our own conversations while the teacher handed out locker numbers. I was desperately trying to think of something to say to Phoebe, when Brianna, a girl I knew from middle school, sat down next to us.

"Tru, I love what you did with your hair this year! Where do you get it highlighted?"

When I said it wasn't highlighted, several other girls joined in to tell me how lucky I was. They went on about how their hair was too frizzy, too straight, wouldn't curl, and so on. Girl talk. And that was it—last year was forgotten. Go figure.

I saw Phoebe rolling her eyes and pulled her into the conversation, asking her how it was possible she had such straight hair when Isaac's was so curly. All the other girls looked enviously at her ebony curtain. Phoebe actually took the bait and explained that they each got one of their parent's hair types.

But when the girls started asking questions about Isaac, talking about him as if he were some rock star, Phoebe rolled her eyes again and shut up. So the chatter moved back to hair and what kind of shampoo everyone used. Honestly, even though Phoebe looked bored, it was nice that everyone wasn't ignoring me or talking about me behind their hands.

By the time my last class arrived, the day had taken a bizarrely positive turn, and my heart felt light as I walked into Mr. Mac's English class. I caught Zander's eye immediately. There was an empty desk next to him. I headed toward the back of the class where he was sitting, but Zena Taylor, wearing a skirt attempting to redefine "mini" as "micro" and a low-cut blouse, slipped into the chair ahead of me, which said a lot for her dexterity because her platform heels were at least five inches. As much as I disliked her, I couldn't help admire the way she got around without killing herself. She immediately leaned toward Zander, ignoring me standing in front of her. A few pens toppled to the floor as several guys pretended to retrieve them all just to get a peek up Zena's skirt. Disgust tightened my lips even as an embarrassed blush spread across my cheeks. Meanwhile, Zena didn't seem to notice them. She was too busy giving Zander another kind of peep show.

"Hi! You're new here." She cast a sultry look toward him, held out her hand to Zander, and then started reeling him in.

"Welcome to Scotts Valley High," she said in her best kitten voice. He shook her hand politely, although it seemed to take an absurd amount of time for his gaze to reach her face. *That ought to teach me.* Boys were all the same.

I cleared my throat, tempted to tell them to get a room. Zena didn't acknowledge me in any way. She just dug her heels in and whipped her long brown hair over her shoulder with the hand that wasn't clinging to Zander's. Her eyelashes dipped in appreciation as she tilted toward him, almost drooling. I needed a vomit bag. *Maybe I should retreat down the aisle and find another way past them,* I thought. I should have known Zena would be in this class. It had all been too perfect.

Okay, everyone has an enemy, and although I wouldn't exactly call her my arch-nemesis, she was definitely on my list of least favorite people. She and her groupies had bullied Ruthie and me all through middle school. Basically, every bad memory of those awkward years involved Zena Taylor, the self-proclaimed gift to Scotts Valley. Gag! I told myself she couldn't help it. What chance did you have with her parents? They were the biggest snobs in town.

However, I loathed any time Zena and her entourage crossed over into my sphere of school. How did she get into this class anyway? Then I remembered that it wasn't AP Lit like I normally would have taken. The school counselor thought I shouldn't push myself with AP classes this year, which meant I was stuck with Zena and her stupid cheerleader friends.

But right now, I felt more peeved that she was sitting next to my blue-eyed guy from lunch, whose introduction had seemed to turn my terrible day around—until now. My distaste must have been visible. Zander's hand was still held captive by Zena, but he was looking at me questioningly, a guilty redness stinging his face. I blinked. Where had this possessiveness come from? Who was I to claim his attention? He looked more like Zena's type anyway—gorgeous. Hoping that I looked indifferent, I smoothed my features and shoved my way over to the aisle on his other side. There was an open seat toward the back. As I tried to squeeze through the narrow aisle, my arm brushed up against him. We both jumped a little from the contact, and he finally escaped Zena's grip. There was that warm hum again. It was not static electricity, but it seemed to cause the same reaction.

"Oh, sorry," I muttered and quickly found my seat. What was wrong with me? Zander's head was twisted around toward me when I settled in and looked up. Next to him, Zena was giving me an "artful" finger gesture behind her back. Whatever. At least Zander didn't seem mad. Actually, one corner of his mouth tilted up, which gave me fluttery heart spasms. He was *really* good-looking.

Aghh! Seriously, what was wrong with me? Had I reached some weird teen hormone stage where I reacted this way to every good-looking guy? I shook my head and I looked over the class. There must be another hunky guy here for me to get flustered about. I spotted Hugh Lawson off to my right. He wore his blond hair overly long, curling around his neck and ears. And he had the cutest freckles over his tanned face. His sky blue eyes and thick eyelashes were the talk of many girls, and I'd seen quite a few comments about him written on the stalls of the girls' bathrooms, which automatically had me glancing down at his butt. I wrenched my eyes back up to his face and gasped. He was looking back at me! He saw me looking at his butt!

My face flushed with embarrassment. He did that head nod thing guys do that seemed to say, "Hey, babe. Yeah, come and get me." Oh my gosh! I quickly turned away. *Okay. No attraction for me there.*

Looking up, I saw Zander glancing between Hugh and me. He caught my eye and tilted his head. When he raised his eyebrow, I knew he was wondering if there was something between Hugh and me. What did he care, anyway? He had just been ogling Zena. Still, I didn't want him or anyone to think I had some crush on Hugh. Flushing again, I shook my head, wanting to bury it in my arms again. Instead, I tried for indifference by pulling out my pen and notebook.

The teacher called everyone's attention to the front of the room, and Zander faced forward. I tried to focus on Mr. Mac, but my eyes kept straying to Zander and Zena (their names even sounded good together!). She attempted to talk with him throughout class, but he didn't seem to hear her. Was he intentionally ignoring her? If so, then he was a better judge of character than the rest of the guys here. Still, I doubted. She always got what she wanted. Since Zena Taylor could claim several relatives as famous actors, this town treated her like royalty. Although her parents were not famous themselves, around here being related was just as good.

Partway through the lecture, I noticed Zander peeking back at me. I couldn't help it. I swung my eyeballs between Zena and him, tilted my own head, and gave him the eyebrow question he'd sent my way earlier. He ducked his head and I saw his shoulders shaking. He quickly caught my eye again, amusement crinkling the corners of his eyes. With the smallest shake of his head, he let me know he wasn't into Zena's scheming. A tiny smile curled up my cheeks as my heart unclenched.

After that, Mr. Mac's Scottish accent quickly enthralled the class, me included. I was excited to learn that we had some Shakespeare on the syllabus—*Romeo and Juliet*, which was one of my favorites. Zena raised her hand to ask if we could see a Romeo and Juliet movie because she wanted to recommend her uncle's performance currently on DVD. I rolled my eyes. I tuned out her sickly sweet voice and let my gaze wander back to Zander. He was looking at something outside the classroom windows. I tried to see what had caught his attention. For the briefest second I thought I saw a blond man all dressed in army-style camouflage clothes standing next to the edge of trees. I blinked and he was gone. Zander was again looking to the front of class. Was it my imagination, or did I just see G.I. Joe and Zander looking at each other? It was so farfetched, I dismissed the notion immediately.

When class finished, Zander zipped out before I, or even Zena, could catch up to him. I sighed and headed to my locker, where Ruthie said she'd meet me after school.

Ruthie was on time, waiting for me at my locker, but she was with someone—Val, her old boyfriend. He looked like he was bringing back the past in a big way. He had her pushed up against the lockers, trapped between his arms. And Ruthie, well, she looked as happy as a kitty in a field of catnip.

I cleared my throat and said, "You are *so* not doing that on my locker."

Val dropped one arm and tried his leer on me. "What? You want some of me, too?"

Well, that did it for Ruthie. She pushed him away and attempted a look of disgust. But I could tell she was into him.

"Need a little help, ladies?" A deep voice sounded behind me. Isaac. He slipped an arm around my shoulders. "Is Valley Girl Val messing with you?" he teased, adding a playful punch on Val's arm. Val winced.

"Hey, Steroid Boy, no need to referee! Ruthie and I were just talking!" He pushed ineffectively at Isaac, which was amusing because Val had it going on in the whole muscle department. How did I know that? Everyone knew because most guys on the football team stripped to their waist after practice and strutted around like peacocks. Val sized up Isaac like he had never seen him before, reluctant respect glinting in his eyes.

I just wanted in my locker, and since Ruthie had moved over, I proceeded to repack my backpack with homework.

"Ha ha, Isaac." Ruthie turned back to Val. "I gotta be home when my brothers get out of school, so I guess I'll see you tomorrow, okay?"

She was giving me a ride home, so I hurried up, glancing distractedly at Val and Ruthie. With a heavy-lidded look thrown over his shoulder, Val took off, immediately yelling at some other guy down the walkway. First day of school was always crazier than normal. And the campus reflected that with kids darting here and there, jammering on about summers and classes, who was who, and sneaking up on each other. Give them a couple weeks of homework, and the exciting atmosphere of the first day would transform to a moody silence broken by locker slams and squeaky sneakers. Okay, that was a little pessimistic, but so true.

The rest of the day was uneventful. Dad was home when Ruthie dropped me off, and I was happy to see that the scratch on the side of his face was almost gone.

And the best part was that there were no night-mares that night, which is not to say that I didn't dream. I did remember two sets of eyes flitting through my subconscious, one brown and one blue.

7

BOBBY

THE NEXT FEW DAYS moved along slowly for me. And the sole reason was that Zander seemed to be avoiding me. I kept seeing him around campus, but he slipped away before I passed him. In class, he sat as far away from me as possible and avoided my gaze. I couldn't help but assume he had heard about me, the "me" from last year. It was inevitable, I guess, but it hurt me like nothing else. He had been a knight in shining armor the first time I met him, as stupid as that sounded, and I had hoped he was going to be different than everyone else.

We didn't see him at lunch, either. All of us wondered where he was, minus Isaac, of course. Phoebe and Isaac were continually bombarded by hopefuls, and Val took up permanent residence next to Ruthie. Isaac kept edging closer to me, making me think perhaps Ruthie had it right and he did like me, but then with all the girls coming by to flirt, well, it was hard to tell. Anyway, my mind kept wandering to Zander, wondering what was up with him.

I also spent a lot of lunch staring around the tables and noticing who was new and how students had changed over the last year. There was the typical jock table, the cheerleader table, the band table, the chess club table, and so on. And then there were the fringe elements, students who didn't seem to belong to any of the groups. I felt like them. I was pretending here at this table full of beautiful and popular kids. I caught the eye of Bobby, sitting two tables away. His gaze skittered away. I remembered him from middle school. He had been pretty popular back then. I wondered what had happened to change him. His hair was messy and overly long. His clothes fit loosely. And he didn't seem to be talking to anyone. Then I remembered. His parents had died tragically in some random drive-by up in Oakland, and Bobby and his brother had been split up between relatives. I felt sick to my stomach imagining losing both my parents. But it had been about four years since his tragedy. Why hadn't I ever reached out to him? Had I ignored him like everyone ignored me last year?

Everyone at my table was busy chatting with someone other than me, so I slipped out and headed over to Bobby. When I sat down across from him, he looked up with wide eyes.

"'sup?" he mumbled.

"Not much. Just bored. Thought you looked bored, too. So..." I started picking at my nail polish. A few tables away, several kids watched us. Whatever, I thought.

Bobby looked around as if to see what was really going on. I followed his gaze to my lunch table. Isaac stared at us, deep grooves in his forehead.

"Looks like your boyfriend can help you with your problem."

"He's not my boyfriend," I said defensively. "Hey, I just wanted to talk."

He raised his eyebrows and smirked. I tried again.

"Um. Well, I just wanted to check on you 'cause...well...I just have this new... Um, I don't know...I just know how tough losing a parent is now and..."

Two bright spots appeared on his cheeks. "Yeah. Sorry about your mom." He frowned, crunching up his soda can and looking for a garbage can.

I cleared my throat. "Thanks. I was probably a total jerk when your parents died. Sorry. I know how much that sucks now. But I was just wondering. Well, you've been dealing with it longer, and...well...I was just wondering how you do it."

Understanding dawned on him and his face closed-in. "Me? I'm not *dealing* with it." His lips thinned. "Look at me. Do I seem like I'm *dealing* with it?"

The anger shocked me. What did I do? But then I saw something else in his eyes. Pain. In fact, I felt it. Unbelievable anguish. It happened four years ago and it was still so much a part of him. Tears welled up in my eyes. I recognized his pain. I knew he was probably fielding the blame. And I hurt thinking that he had been feeling this way for so long. No wonder he looked so bad. Was I going to be this messed up four years from now? What was there to hope for? I brushed away a runaway tear.

Bobby noticed and blanched, regret pulling his face down, trying to capture my gaze. "I'm sorry. It's still fresh for you, but I'm the last person you want to ask for advice."

He rose to leave, but I grabbed his hand braced on the table, stopping his exit. He sighed and sat back down, glaring at me again. I wanted him to feel happy, like he used to be. No one should feel like this for as long as he had.

"Bobby. I remember you in Mrs. Frost's history class way back in seventh grade. You were hilarious and happy and really, really fun. I wish you could be that person again." I said it so fervently, Bobby's eyes shifted off to one side and then back to mine. They were angry and sorrowful. But now I saw hope in them, too. I squeezed his fingers, thinking that he deserved to get over this, that his parents would have wanted him to be happy, that his brother needed him to be better.

"Bobby," I insisted. "It will get better." My hand felt warm, but I continued, gripping his fingers tighter. "You have to be better. Daniel is your younger brother, right?"

He nodded, blankly. I remembered that Daniel had been a couple years younger. I wondered where he was.

"He needs you," I said, not knowing where that came from, but feeling that it was true. "You *will* be better." Bobby's eyes seemed to glow. I hoped I hadn't made him cry.

I pulled my hand away, suddenly feeling tired, but Bobby grabbed it back and leaned in closely. I could definitely see the moisture in his eyes now.

"You're right, Tru. I'll do it. I'll call him tonight." He smiled. "Hey, are you all right?"

I smiled back, too weary to reply. I was feeling so tired, I thought about resting my head on the table. I felt like I might fall over, actually. No. I didn't want to pass out in front of all these people. I gripped the edge of the table just as an arm curled around my shoulders. I turned to see blue eyes. Zander. And then I felt that wonderful hum.

"Sorry, Bobby. I feel a little weird. I-I just need to get out of here." I tried to stand up. Zander supported me and the dizziness passed.

"Wow. Weird head rush, I guess. I should have eaten more for lunch." I laughed at myself. Zander still hadn't said anything, but he scowled at Bobby.

"Hey, man, I didn't do anything."

Zander walked me toward the closest building, sheltering me from student eyes with an arm around my shoulder. By the time we got to the girls' restroom, I felt almost normal.

I pushed away from Zander, laughing hollowly. "Sorry about that. Thanks for keeping me upright."

"What just happened?" he asked point blank.

My eyebrows leaped. He acted like I had done something wrong. "I don't know. Maybe I ate something bad. Maybe I didn't eat enough?"

"Tru!" a voice called down the hall. It was Isaac. Great. By the time he caught up to me, Zander had slipped away. Strange. I tried to shrug off the feeling of disappointment.

Isaac growled during my explanation, and I felt like laughing at him. Seriously, he could be really funny sometimes. I felt tired but for some reason giddy, despite the whole Isaac/Zander weirdfest. I saw Bobby in the hall later that day, and he gave me a smile and a wave, which made me smile hugely back at him. I hoped that I had made a new friend.

8

TIGHT PLACES

AFTER SCHOOL I WAITED for Ruthie to do her flirty goodbye thing with Val before we took off. Isaac walked up to us flashing his commercial smile.

"Hey, Ruthie," said Isaac, "can you give Phoebe and me a lift to our mom's shop?" His mom ran a jewelry counter inside a clothing store that was kind of on the way home for Ruthie.

"Sure, but it'll be tight because I've got Tru, too."

"No prob," replied Isaac. "And here's Phoebe, right on time."

Phoebe glared at Isaac, who just stared back. It was like they were having a silent conversation.

Ruthie leaned over to me and whispered, "It's a twin thing, I think. They do that all the time. Used to freak me out."

Whatever the problem was, they snapped out of it. We looked at them expectantly, but Isaac just smiled and herded us down the hall, saying, "Come on, ladies, let's go!"

As we got close to the car, Phoebe yelled, "Shotgun," unenthusiastically.

"Oh, come on! I don't think Isaac is going to fit in the back of a mini by himself, let alone with me!" I snickered.

Phoebe just raised an eyebrow. "You'd be surprised what he can do when motiva—" Isaac coughed awkwardly. "And since I'm taking the front," she continued in a monotone voice, "he has no choice."

"Hmmm," mused Ruthie, looking between the two.

"What?" I said.

"Later," she promised.

Well, this will be interesting, I thought. We dumped our backpacks in the trunk and Isaac proceeded to squeeze in the backseat—it was like Cirque du Soleil. I heard a chuckle in the distance and saw Zander walking toward a green truck and watching Isaac. Behind the wheel sat the man I thought I'd seen through our classroom window the first day of school. G.I. Joe guy. Guess I didn't imagine him. Strange, though. He was glaring at Zander. What was up with him? He looked too young to be Zander's father, maybe twenty-something. He didn't look anything like him, so I doubted he was a sibling. He sure did not seem to appreciate the humor of our situation like Zander did.

"Okay. You next, Tru," said Isaac. I looked in and thought that my jeans alone would have trouble fitting in there. I didn't know how I was going to manage all of me.

"Uh..." I said doubtfully.

"Come on, you can fit," he urged, holding out his hand.

I braced one hand on the doorframe and gave him my other. I landed in his lap.

"Oh!" I gasped. I looked up at him and then out the window behind him. The green truck was passing us and now Zander had a scowl on his face. Maybe the two *could* be brothers, I thought, amending my earlier observation.

I scrambled into my seat. "I don't think I can get my seat belt on," I squeaked.

Eventually, I was secured and squished up next to Isaac, the two of us as close as two stalks of celery. I could have sworn there was space on the other side of him, but I guess he needed room for his giant muscle arms.

Isaac had his arm around the back of my seat. As uncomfortable as I was, smashed into the backseat, I tried not to laugh at how much worse he looked. Ruthie had put the top down so his head wouldn't wrench a hole through it, but his legs were folded awkwardly to the side and took up half of my legroom. I tried to put some space between us. The breeze was blowing my hair all over the place, so I reached up with both hands to try and confine it.

"Allow me," said Isaac chivalrously as he pulled his arm over the headrest and trapped my hair under it. It worked to keep my hair from flying out of the car, but it pulled me closer to him and I became nestled up against his side once again. It was cozier than I wanted but comfortable, so I just went with it.

I caught Ruthie's eyes in the mirror. She wiggled her eyebrows suggestively. I giggled.

"What's so funny?" asked Isaac, leaning down to my ear, his breath tickling me.

Couldn't he see the humor in this? "Duh! Us in this backseat!" I replied bluntly.

"Are you uncomfortable?" he asked.

"Not really, but *you* have to be!" I smacked his knee, which wasn't that far from my face. "How can you stand this?" I laughed.

He let loose a snort and grinned. "I'm okay."

Phoebe turned back to us and smirked. "Yeah, don't worry about him."

Isaac scowled back.

Whatever, I thought. We were almost to the store. Ruthie whipped into the parking lot and came to a snappy stop that would have thrown me into her seat if I weren't wedged tightly under Isaac's arm.

"All giants out of my car," announced Ruthie. Phoebe threw her a dirty look.

"Well, seriously, girl!" defended Ruthie. "I go away for two months and you're suddenly colossal big. I swear, all my friends are supermodel height while I'm shortness defined."

"Drama much?" replied Phoebe. "Besides, I've reduced my dating pool by 80 percent. Plus, you get to wear whatever heels you want and no worries. So not feeling sorry for you."

"Huh. You're right!" agreed Ruthie, pacified now that she thought she had one up on Phoebe. "Now move your mammoth butts out of here, folks. I'm not kidding, I've got to get home!" Luckily, Phoebe didn't take offense and stepped out of the car.

"Harsh, Ruthie," I said as I tried to extricate myself from Isaac.

As soon as Phoebe was out, Isaac pushed up her seat and started wiggling free himself. As he stood up, he grabbed me around the waist and lifted me out. His fingers dug into my sides, and I couldn't help it when I literally convulsed, my body twisting away from him.

"Errr...aahhh...stop!" I would have dropped to the pavement if he hadn't been quick enough to catch me.

He pulled me up close and whispered, "Ticklish, eh?"

I shoved him away with a "No!" I hated it when people found out how ticklish I was and thought, "Oh, wouldn't it be fun to tickle her!" It wasn't fun for me, it was torture!

Isaac backed away, hands up. "Okay, okay! No tickling." He still smirked.

Ruthie revved the car. "Going. Now!"

"K!" I said. A quick farewell wave, and we were off.

Ruthie was a little desperate to get home, so we got to my house in record time, her ranting about her parents' stupid rules most of the way. I barely had time to get the scoop on her and Val. She'd still been crushing on him for years. I had no idea. She was a little defensive, probably because she had talked smack about him for years. And I'd believed it this whole time. Then she complained about most of her teachers and how little time she had that night to finish the mountain of homework that should never be allowed on the first week of school.

When she got like this, it was better to just let her vent. It was a Ruthie bubble that just got bigger and bigger until it popped and then she could see everyone else again. But it didn't bother me today.

Dad's car was in the driveway and I could smell a roast in the Crockpot as soon as I opened the front door. We'd starve to death without a Crockpot.

"I'm home!" I yelled.

Dad's head popped out of his office. "Hey, how was school, honey?" He had a hopeful, yet veiled look on his face. Probably expecting the worst. He had been giving me some space since school started.

"Not bad, really."

A smile spread across his face, relief pulling it wide. "That's wonderful! Come on in and tell me all about it."

My breath hitched. Again, I didn't want to rehash the last few days; they had been bizarre and wonderful and normal all at the same time. What did he expect me to say? It was *school!* How could I get out of this? My heavy backpack gave me an idea. I let it pull me over a little as if it were filled with rocks.

"Actually, I don't have time. The principal is shooting for a higher API score again. And the teachers all dumped on us already. I've gotta get started on it now, or I'll never finish tonight."

"Oh, okay, honey. We'll catch up later. Besides, I'm a little overloaded with work right now. Our project fell way behind and the bosses are screaming for miracles." He sighed. "I may be in the office a lot tomorrow and next week."

"That's okay, Dad. I'm going to be buried anyway, if the next week is anything like this one." Not true, because frankly, my classes this year weren't that hard. But it got me out of talking about my day like kindergarten sharing time. Besides, I was glad Dad's work was busy. Dad loved his job, which is why he wasn't retired completely yet. And he was way good at it, too. That's what Mom used to say. She would have seen right through me. I missed her right now. Dad must have noticed something in my face because he pulled me into a hug.

"Love you, Tru Lee and always," he whispered. He always said that as a little joke. My middle name is Lee. Yep, pretty lame.

"Not breathing." That was my little hint that I was ready for the hug to be over. He laughed and sent me off.

HOURS LATER, I JUMPED with a strangled gasp as Dad popped his head in and said "Good Night, Honey!"

"Geez! You almost gave me a heart attack!"

He chuckled. "Sorry, I thought you were studying."

"I was!" I gestured to the messy assortment of textbooks and paper across my desk.

I ran my hands over my face, trying to shake off the sleep. One second I was sitting at my desk with a textbook cracked open, staring out my bedroom window at the wild tomato plants that had started by themselves from my mom's old garden, and next I was almost falling out of my chair in fright.

"Oh, pardon me!" he said gallantly. "That osmosis thing never worked for me. But better luck to you. And, sweet dreams!" Dad ducked out before I could toss a pillow his way.

"Goodnight, Dad!" I yelled before turning back to my untidy desk.

Bits of a dream swam around my mind. It hadn't been scary. It was mostly a memory, I think. When I was a little girl, Mom and I planted a garden from seeds. I checked on the rounded rows of dirt almost hourly, impatiently waiting for them to sprout. Mom finally told me to leave them alone so they could sleep. So I decided to take a nap out there in the garden. I bedded down on some patio chair cushions with my fluffy toy dog and a blanket.

When Dad picked me up to carry me into the house, he asked, "How's my little gardener?"

I replied, "I'm no gardener, I'm a sleeper. I'm not sprouted yet."

Dad had laughed at that back then, just like he'd been laughing at me now. It was so surreal.

Why had I remembered that? Had it really happened? The phrase "I'm a sleeper" kept repeating in my head, distracting me. Finally, I resorted to my headphones, the music blocking out annoying thoughts and allowing me to focus on homework. If luck was on my side, I'd get to sleep for real by midnight.

9

SMOOCH

BEFORE I KNEW IT, I was opening my eyes to Friday morning. For a moment, I felt something was amiss. Then I realized what it was—no nightmares! They had been plaguing me on and off this week. Fortunately they hadn't been bad enough to wake Dad.

I sent a heartfelt thank you out into the great unknown to whomever or whatever had helped me, because I was really grateful for the uninterrupted night of sleep. Sure enough, the mirror reflected that sleep really could do miracles.

Dad was already gone. He took off early so he wouldn't be stuck in the traffic winding through the mountains toward Silicon Valley, where his office was located. It was a horrible commute. A Post-it note stuck to the front door:

Have a great day, Tru!
Lunch in the fridge!
Love, Dad

I smiled.

Ruthie chatted all the way to school about lame little brothers and how late she stayed up to finish homework. She was still stuck in her bubble.

School was uneventful, and I thought about Bobby all morning, wondering how he was feeling.

By the time lunch rolled around, I eagerly made my way to our table, noticing Bobby at a new table talking with a group of kids. He looked a lot better and it made me smile as I speculated about which Isaac/Phoebe groupies would be invading today. Ruthie, Phoebe, and Isaac were already there. Val walked up at the same time as I did, squeezing in between the two girls. Ruthie seemed happy about it, but Phoebe gave him a glare that was totally wasted because he was all about Ruthie. Isaac pulled me down next to him, making me feel wanted, which warmed my heart just a little.

"Hey there, Parker."

"Hey back," I replied, knocking my shoulder into his arm. He looked awesome in his ratty jeans and white

T-shirt. His curly hair stuck up all over the place. I smiled nervously.

Phoebe glanced from Isaac and me to Ruthie and Val, distaste clear on her face.

"Where's Zander lately?" she asked. Everyone shrugged.

"I don't know," I answered, although she hadn't directed the question at anyone in particular.

"Oh, here he comes," she asserted, the sparkle back in her eyes. I sighed. Perfect. I'm not sure at what point I considered myself actually in the running to gain Zander's attention. And I wasn't sure if I even wanted it with all the girls drooling after him. It would be a constant battle.

Isaac was in the middle of stuffing his face, but somehow he worked in a scowl at his sister. He sat up straighter and inched closer to me.

I peeked in the direction of Phoebe's gaze and locked on to Zander's midnight blue eyes. But he was looking at Phoebe, who lit up at the attention. Although there was plenty of room next to me, he squeezed into the spot on the other side of Phoebe. Val protested but he and Ruthie shifted down to make room. Phoebe smiled beautifully, her pearly white teeth sparkling, and scooted closer to me to give Zander some more space.

I felt like I had been slapped. I had no reason to expect him to cozy up to me, especially with Isaac next to me, but I still felt hurt. I ducked my head, but not before I saw Isaac throw Zander a look of dislike. What now? His sister couldn't like someone?

Why did my eyes feel all watery? How stupid was I? Seriously! I had Isaac's undivided attention and half the quad of girls staring at me with jealousy. Well, they could be staring at Phoebe—there were all kinds of reasons to be jealous there, but— Gahhh! I was being dumb and immature and really emotional, just like a girl. *Suck it up, Parker!* That made me think of Isaac and our drama class. I really needed some of those acting skills right now. I could do this.

I fixed a bored look on my face, straightened my spine, and thought: *I don't give a shirtless shanghaied shaman about what Zander thinks of me or whomever the freak he likes!*

Then I looked up and right into those stellar blues. My mask slipped just for a second because he actually had a contrite expression on his face. What up?

Phoebe struck up a conversation just for the two of them, obviously, because I could barely hear her. I turned to Isaac, who was swigging down his bottle of milk. He caught my look and lowered the bottle. I smiled because he was just so dopey-looking with that little milk mustache. Before he could read too much into my smile, I motioned to his upper lip and then his milk, but he just smiled wider. And then he leaned in and threatened to smooch me.

I automatically jumped out of my seat, laughing, because he looked like he just might do it, but he had hold of my arm. I squealed, managing to slip free. Something about a girl running from a boy—boys were such dogs. It just always seems to make them chase you more. But running was a reflex I couldn't change. I really didn't want milk all over me. And, honestly, I wasn't that comfortable with him laying one on me in front of my lunch table or the whole school. Unfortunately, as I passed one of the tables near the edge of the quad, Hugh Lawson snagged me, pulled my arms behind my back, and held me by the waist. I didn't think things could get worse, but they did.

"Hey, Isaac! Caught someone for you!" He laughed evilly. Isaac was on me in a second, grabbing me from Hugh's arms. Ignoring my pleas, he laid one on me, milk and all. And it wasn't bad, just weird because I knew everyone was staring. Hugh released me, cackling. The whole quad was laughing and pointing at me.

I froze. This was way too much like my outcast memories of last year.

Isaac caught on before anyone else noticed my freaked-out state. As quick as lightning, he threw me over his shoulder and hauled me around the nearest building. Plopping me down on the pavement against a wall of lockers, he crouched down to cradle my face. He wiped the milk from both of us.

"Tru, I'm really, really sorry if that hurt you in any way. I was just having fun."

I knew that already, and I totally knew I was blowing things out of proportion. I smiled regretfully.

"It's okay. I don't know what happened to me. It just felt a little like last year with everyone staring. Sorry."

"They weren't really laughing at you, you know. It was just fun. I won't be surprised if we've started something. At the very least, I bet more of them will be buying milk."

A laugh forced its way out of me. "Yeah, we could have been a commercial for milk."

He hooted, the sound booming down the corridor. "Hey. I'm going to go grab our stuff and be right back, okay? Unless you want to go back to the table?"

"No, thanks. I'm fine here."

"K. Be right back."

I heard the cheers as he ran across the quad. *Let the rumors begin,* I thought. I was grateful for my shady corner, because it kept everyone on the edge of the quad from seeing me.

So, my first kiss was in front of the whole school, and it was from the milky mouth of Hottie Efoti. My conflicting thoughts turned to Zander. What had he thought of this? Was he thinking the same as half the guys out there and considering joining the milky mouth crowd, with Phoebe? Again, why did I care? He was into her and all her graceful beauty, and why shouldn't he be?

Seconds later, Isaac skidded over to me and sat down to finish his lunch. He distracted me with the gossip he had heard that morning. The rest of lunch flew by.

STILL FEELING SNUBBED BY Zander by the time English arrived, I prepared to write Zander off my list of acquaintances and determined to sit as far from him as possible.

I pulled into class with time to spare and spotted an empty chair on the far left of class, near the windows. Zander didn't seem to be anywhere in sight, but as I settled in, I heard Zena's loud whisper.

"He's sooo hot!"

A bevy of whispers followed.

No need to look up. It had to be Zander. *Please, please don't sit behind me,* I prayed. I buried my face in the textbook and sent up another desperate plea. Footsteps neared me, but I didn't look up.

A backpack thudded against the floor.

"Hey, Tru." Yes, Zander had picked the seat behind me. Why? There had to be at least eight other seats further away! I tried for a calming breath, but it came out ragged. I couldn't ignore him. He would guess something was up, and then he would guess that I was into him. And that could NOT happen. *Calm. Calm. Act normal,* I counseled myself.

I turned around with a fake smile plastered on my face.

"Hi Zander!" I cringed at the higher pitch to my voice.

He stared at me, eyebrows drawn together.

"You okay?" he asked.

Great. He thought there was something wrong. And if he noticed that, then he'd wonder what it was, and then he'd rewind the day to lunch and realize the looks I gave him were pathetic and stalker-ish.

"Yeah, sure!" I assured him. "What's up?"

"Hey, Zander!" breathed Zena. *Speaking of stalkers,* I thought. Looks like she'd packed up her backpack and moved closer to Zander. His jaw tightened.

"Zena," he said. And that's all he said. It looked like he was bent on ignoring her the rest of class. I turned toward the front just as Mr. Mac welcomed everyone.

As soon as the bell rang, Zena and her groupies overwhelmed Zander. They actually shoved me out of the way as I stood up to collect my things. Wow. Being irresistible was not what it was cracked up to be. I met Zander's scowling eyes over the girls' heads and shook my head at his frustration. Besides, why was he acting like he wanted to hang out all of a sudden? He was hot and cold and most certainly bad for me. I hurried out of class.

Today it was just Ruthie and me on the way home. We stopped for frozen yogurt and I couldn't resist telling her about Zander's fan club attack. She choked on her water.

I think I actually heard her self-absorbed bubble pop.

"No way!"

"Yep!"

"That's awesome. About time someone didn't fall for her."

"Yeah," I said. "He's obviously into Phoebe, anyway. She could kick Zena's butt, I think. Should get interesting."

"Huh? He likes Phoebe? Where did you hear that?"

"Well, duh! Didn't you see them at lunch?"

"Lunch... Yeah...I was there... How did I miss it? What did you see?"

"He sat by her, closely." It sounded lame, but I knew I was right.

"Oh yeah! Close sitting!" she said sarcastically. "That sure gave it away!" She snickered. "Really. Anyway, it's not like he was chasing her down and kissing her in front of the whole school!" she sputtered. "That was awesome, by the way!"

I blushed, fresh embarrassment washing over me.

"I thought it was weird."

"Seriously? Believe me, your reputation score went up about fifty points with that stunt, especially when he went all caveman and dragged you off to a dark corner. Ahhh! Young love." She sighed loudly.

"No, really it wasn't like that. At least not for me."

"Girlfriend, you are being handed a Get-Out-of-Jail-Free card. After last year, you need this kind of cred.

Isaac is way up there on the popular scale—big points for you—and he's bringing you up there with him. This is what I was talking about before! No one is going to remember last year after a few more episodes in the Isaac and Tru series. And the more public, the faster this is going to happen. Seriously, you are so lucky! It's like you have your own guardian angel/cupid working for you. It's a beautiful thing. Man! I love this stuff!" She dipped her spoon into her marshmallow-covered chocolate yogurt and licked it clean, ecstasy causing her eyeballs to roll backward.

I giggled. She was so over the top, I couldn't stay worried. I pushed that guilty feeling into a corner and ignored it. So, Zander was out and Isaac was in. Moving on. Why did my stomach start to ache?

10

New Friends

I WOKE UP SATURDAY morning exhausted. Another night of dreaming. But I didn't remember much. Just bits and pieces. Back to the cavemen people. Something about families attacking one another, a woman with seven wolves howling around her, and glowing red eyes. It was just creepy. No wonder I slept poorly.

I decided to make Dad breakfast for a change, so I hustled into the kitchen in my PJs and took out some bacon and hash browns. I got those started before mixing up the eggs. The tediousness of my actions was soothing and soon erased the eerie feeling from my dreams. It didn't take long for Dad to smell the food. Waking up to bacon was the best.

Dad and I spent the day cleaning and sprucing up the place. It was long overdue and we rewarded ourselves with pizza and a movie that night. It felt nice, normal. No school drama, no boy problems, and no strange wolf appearances. For the first time since Mom died, it seemed that our life would, indeed, get better. This was us moving on. It was sad but hopeful. I decided it was a good thing. I thought about Bobby and hoped that he was doing okay. He sure seemed happier at school yesterday.

I spent the next day completing all my homework and talking to Ruthie on the phone. She filled me in on the latest horrors of having younger brothers and parents who make you do chores for gas money. All I could do was shake my head and listen. She promised chocolate cupcakes for being such a great friend. That was probably the 100th time she'd said that, and no cupcakes had appeared as of yet. Someday, I was going to receive a houseful of them all at the same time, or so I could dream.

The best part of the weekend was the call I got from Bobby. I don't know how he got my number, but I was pleasantly surprised to hear his voice. He wanted to thank me for urging him to visit his brother. His brother had just started a different high school and he hated it. He had been super happy to hear from his big brother, and they hung out all weekend. I could have sworn Bobby got choked up talking about it, and it made me all warm inside when I realized I had really helped him.

It reminded me of my summer at the rec center. Teaching the kids there had really turned my year around. I wish I could have seen Uncle Ira more often. I hadn't seen him since he got me the job. I was told he was working out of the country for a while.

Both Saturday and Sunday nights were blissfully nightmare-free. So Monday morning began with plenty of beauty sleep, and Ruthie surprised me with a plate full of chocolate cupcakes topped with fluffy chocolate icing. They didn't even last to first bell. Isaac and Phoebe caught up with us in the parking lot swearing that they smelled chocolate, so we had to pull out the plate and share. Between the four of us, and Val (Ruthie had texted him to hurry over if he wanted one), they were gone in a jiffy. We walked into class on a chocolate high. It was a great way to start the day.

Our schedule had been adjusted to make time for an assembly right before lunch. There would be no seventh period. I wondered if I would see Zander at lunch today since we didn't have English.

Ruthie and I agreed to meet at my locker and head to the gym together. We arrived just in time to grab a seat near the end of the bleachers. Isaac stood halfway across the floor, surrounded by a swarm of girls, but he was looking in our direction. He pulled away from them to head over, but someone beat him to us.

Zander. I knew it was him even before I turned. The entire side of my body sizzled.

"Hey," he said.

Ruthie reached across me to give him a high-five like they were buddies. I just mumbled "hey," having no clue how to react to him. Suddenly Isaac loomed over us, thunder on his face. Zander didn't seem to notice as he speculated what the assembly was about, and Isaac was forced to grab the space next to Ruthie. Suddenly, the football team ran into the gym dressed as cheerleaders. Everyone went wild, including Ruthie, who jumped up screaming. Isaac took the opportunity to squeeze Ruthie over and sit by me. She didn't seem to mind, sneaking in a quick wink at me. Somehow, with all the mayhem going on, Phoebe wedged in next to Ruthie, and they huddled together giggling about the guys in vests and skirts that were too small for them.

While Phoebe and Ruthie were getting into the spirit of the assembly, I was left in Awkwardville between Isaac and Zander.

Predictably, the next crew to run in was the cheerleading team dressed in football jerseys and gear. The assembly was mostly an advertisement for Homecoming next month, laced with the annual speeches on school rules and school pride. Ruthie screamed for Val as he leaped and pounded his pom-poms together. He was ridiculous, but then, so was she.

It was too loud most of the time to talk to each other, but after the football players and cheerleaders left and the principal began droning on about parking lot behavior, Zander leaned in to ask me about an English assignment. It was a little surreal and extremely uncomfortable since I could feel Isaac tense up beside me. As soon as he could work in a comment, I was turned toward him. It was like a Ping Pong game, and I was the ball. To heighten my discomfort, the vibrations coming off Zander every time our skin touched made it difficult for me to focus on what Isaac said. I probably sounded super lame.

Thankfully, the assembly didn't last too long and then it was lunchtime. I darted off to my locker to grab lunch, at the same time wondering if Zander would be sitting with us again. I didn't think I could take any more weirdness between Isaac and him, so I considered my options.

A solution presented itself when Bobby caught up with me and invited me to sit with him and some old friends. I was so pleased to hear that he was hanging with other people again, and I wanted to support the new him, so I agreed. Plus, it solved my little lunch dilemma. I doubted Ruthie would care. She and Val would be all over each other anyway. I sent her a quick text so she wouldn't wonder and give me crap about it later.

Bobby's friends huddled around a table at the far edge of the quad, which was completely opposite my regular table. Shrina, Dara, James, and someone I didn't recognize were already seated. I'd never really had much to do with them before, mostly because our interests hadn't ever crossed. They were what I called band geeks. I'd forgotten that Bobby was into music.

Shrina was smiling brightly at Bobby, and I thought I caught a glimpse of something in her eyes. Dara and James looked like Siamese twins eating from the same lunch bag. The other kid, a guy with wavy black hair that covered most of his face, held a guitar.

"Hi guys," announced Bobby. "You remember Tru?" The girls welcomed me with friendly hellos. The guys gave me nods.

"Tru, you know Shrina, right? And Dara and James?"

Bobby slid into the bench next to Shrina, who smiled and lowered her long black eyelashes. She was cute and perhaps a little into Bobby. I remembered she had an Indian accent.

"Yeah," I said. "You and I got paired up for wheelbarrow racing at Hanh Nguyen's birthday party in seventh grade, right?"

"Oh my gosh! I forgot about that. I was so horrible, but we still won!" She laughed.

"And, then there's Dara and James—they were in Mrs. Skinner's science class with us. When we dissected frogs?" Bobby continued the introductions.

"Sure." I smiled. "Hated the frogs, though."

"Same here," said Dara, her blue eyes crinkling at the corners. James just grunted and nodded his head.

"And here's Dante." Bobby nodded toward the guitarist. "He moved here from San Francisco this summer. He's killer with the guitar."

"Wow," I said. Dante acknowledged our awe with a few light strokes on the guitar. I chuckled. Dante stared back at me with a speculative look in his eyes. My laughter died away as an uneasy feeling swept over me. But then he smiled, revealing two dimples, one in each cheek, a phenomenon Ruthie liked to label a "double D boy." I smiled back at him.

I wondered when Bobby had made friends with this group. Shrina revealed that they had been trying to coax him into their music group for a while, and finally, Bobby had agreed. She beamed as she explained. Definitely something going on between the two of them. They made a cute couple.

And that's how I avoided the uncomfortable lunch table across the quad. Although I couldn't avoid Isaac or Zander in our classes, they were a lot easier to handle one-on-one.

Just before the bell rang, everyone at the table took off except Dante. I was reaching for my backpack when he stopped me.

"That was quite a trick, what you did for Bobby," he said.

"Excuse me?"

"Yeah, Bobby was a week away from committing suicide, and bam! Suddenly he's calling his brother and making friends. Damn miracle, wouldn't you say?"

Suicide? What was he suggesting? "What are you talking about?"

With his eyebrows raised, he pondered, "You don't even know, do you?" He looked over my shoulder and quickly muttered, "Idimmu, you're idimmu."

I could barely hear him. "What? I'm a dummy?"

He rolled his eyes. "We'll have to talk later. But don't worry, I'll keep your secret." And he took off.

Just as I was wondering why he had left so quickly and what drugs he was taking, Isaac plopped down next to me.

"Hey. Is he bothering you?" He looked hopeful.

I just shook my head, "No. But he is strange."

Isaac laughed. "Yeah, could have told you that myself. He's in algebra with me. Let's get to class." He grabbed my backpack, and with his on one shoulder and mine on the other, we took off to drama.

11

HOMECOMING

AFTER SCHOOL ISAAC AND Phoebe begged another ride to their mom's shop from Ruthie, and once again, I found myself smashed up next to Isaac in the backseat.

Ruthie decided to drop me off first. As we pulled into my driveway, I noticed Dad's truck was missing, and I remembered that he would be working late a lot this week.

Phoebe stepped out and helped to extract me from the backseat. With surprising strength, she whisked me out and onto the driveway.

"Geez! You guys are turning my cute car into a sideshow!" Ruthie declared.

"It's like a clown car." I chuckled.

We were still cracking clown jokes as I pulled out my backpack. Suddenly, Phoebe and Isaac froze and gave each other one of their twin looks.

"Oh for pork's sake, what's wrong now?" exclaimed Ruthie impatiently. She glanced at her car clock, obviously worried about getting home on time. I knew she didn't want to risk the sweet deal she had with her parents, who were threatening to take her car away if she didn't get home on time.

"Tru, can I use your bathroom before I go?" asked Phoebe. "I hate using the restroom at the store."

"Seriously?" complained Ruthie.

"Uh...sure," I said, grateful that Dad and I had cleaned over the weekend.

As we walked through the front door, we heard Isaac say, "I don't think I can take this car anymore."

I looked back to see him shimmying out of the car and grabbing for the backpacks.

"Phew!" he huffed. "I think I'd prefer to walk. We'll hoof it the rest of the way, Ruthie, and you can get home in time."

I looked at Phoebe. "You okay with walking the rest of the way?" I asked, continuing inside.

She waved away my concern. "We hike all the time. Not a big deal." She glanced around the living room, her nostrils flaring. I could have sworn she was sniffing the air. She noticed my bewilderment.

"So...nice place! Smells good in here. Is that the kitchen?" She walked ahead of me. I was trying to smell something, but it just smelled like "vacant house" to me. I made a mental note to buy some room spray.

Make yourself right at home, I thought, following her. Out of the corner of my eye, I saw movement in the backyard.

"Hey! Someone's in the backyard." My heart racing, I rushed over to the kitchen window.

"Oh, that's just Isaac," Phoebe said. "He's probably checking out your yard."

What the heck? I was starting to feel a little invaded by the twins.

"What's he doing out there?" I headed to the back door. Phoebe tried to head me off. This was getting too weird, and I quickly moved around her and out the door.

"Isaac!" I yelled, exasperated. "What are you doing?"

He whirled around, startled. He flashed a smile.

"Man! You caught me! I was going to surprise Phoebe when she walked by," he explained. "I love to mess with her."

"Yeah," she shot back. "Nice try, brother."

Isaac's lips tightened as he glanced around. I looked, too. Our backyard wasn't very pretty these days.

"How can you stand such close neighbors?" complained Isaac, looking toward the back fence.

"What? Who doesn't have neighbors? Anyway, it's not like you get to pick them," I said.

"Actually," inserted Phoebe, "we live way out in the woods for that very reason. We're surrounded by trees and—no neighbors."

"Really? That sounds pretty cool. But doesn't it get creepy with all the fog we get?" I wasn't sure if I'd like it in the woods on a foggy day, which we had in abundance this close to the coast, but otherwise, the privacy would be refreshing. One of our neighbors had a live mariachi band playing at least once a month. Enough said.

"Nah," denied Isaac. "We love it out there. Lots of space to run around..."

"Yeah, I bet capture the flag would be awesome at your place!" I agreed.

"Absolutely! You should come out there some time," he said. Phoebe was looking at the house and I remembered that she needed to use the restroom.

"Oh, Phoebe. Bathroom is at the end of the hall. Can't miss it."

"What?" she said. "Oh yeah, thanks." She headed back into the house.

Isaac and I sat down at the patio table to wait. He overwhelmed our small furniture. It was a wonder he could even fit in the chair.

"So, why aren't you playing football this year?" I asked. His sheer size would be an asset to the team.

He frowned. "Believe it or not, my parents won't let me."

"Are you serious? Why?"

"Um, they're afraid I'm going to break something?" He looked amused now.

That sent me into a laughing fit. "Wow. And I thought my parents were overprotective! That's just ridiculous."

"I know. It's pretty annoying sometimes." He smiled down at me, and I blushed at the warmth in his brown eyes.

"Speaking of football," he continued, "I can't believe Homecoming is coming up already."

"Oh, yeah. Bizarre, huh?" Where was this going? Alarm bells were going off. Was he going to ask me out? Part of me wanted him to ask me. I had never gone to Homecoming, and it would go a long way to reviving me from my zombie reputation, especially if I went with him. I imagined him in a tux, and it was mouth-watering. Still, when I looked deep down in that secret place, I couldn't help but imagine another boy in a tux.

Isaac fidgeted with his leather bracelet before looking back at me.

"I guess it's still early, but, uh, are you going with anyone yet?" he said.

"No." My heart was pounding.

He smiled that dental commercial smile again. I remembered his milky kiss. “How about coming with me, then?”

“Okay,” I said, lost in the brilliance of the moment. I was giddy. Someone asked me to Homecoming—on the second week of school! I couldn't wait to tell Ruthie.

“Awesome!” He wrapped his hand in mine, a wide smile splitting his face. He leaned in closer.

All I could think was *Wait just a minute! What's happening?* But then he suddenly pulled back with a slight scowl. I breathed a sigh of relief.

“Well, guess I should get going, then.” He slung his backpack over his shoulder.

“What about Phoebe?” I asked. But before I even finished my question, she was stepping out the back door, as if on cue.

“Yeah, we'll just head out your side gate, Tru.” Phoebe took off with Isaac, and I just waved goodbye, absently.

Making eye contact one last time, a new eagerness in his gaze, Isaac dipped his head in goodbye. “See you at lunch tomorrow!”

Then they were gone. It felt—I don't know—a little orchestrated. But I smiled at my silliness. Isaac was so sweet. And yet, why did I feel slightly ill?

I looked around our backyard again. There was just a small patch of grass next to Mom's garden. Dad was barely keeping it alive. I wondered how long it would last. Mom had been raised in the farming belt of California. Even though the coastal town of Scotts Valley was wooded and often covered in fog, she still managed to produce a flourishing garden. Dad had planted one this summer in her memory. By some miracle, the tomatoes were still growing. I walked closer to pick some of the ripe ones. That's when I noticed the footprints—from a dog, I thought. But, they were huge! I followed them around the dirt. They were all over the backyard. Although it seemed ages ago, I recalled the wolf I'd seen on the way to school. What was going on? Shivering, I hurried into the house and locked the doors.

That night I finally dreamed about my mom. Dad and Uncle Ira were in it, too. It had that nostalgic quality, like a filter on a camera lens.

Uncle Ira sat on the couch, in our old living room. Only all the furniture was the old stuff we got rid of years and years ago. He looked sad, but my parents gazed at a little three-year-old who was hugging Uncle Ira's leg, fiercely. They were enraptured.

I was viewing the scene from a distance, but I knew the little kid was me—I had photos. I must have been about three years old. Mom seemed to be coaxing the girl toward her.

"Come here, honey. We're going to be great friends." She had that sweet schoolteacher voice going. All the kids had loved her as their teacher. And the

voice worked on the child, who finally relinquished her anchor and let Mom pull her into her lap. Little me gazed up at her, tears still in her eyes.

"My, you look just like my baby pictures, don't you," Mom said with wonder.

"That's what Caroline always said. She really wanted you two to meet," said Uncle Ira. "But, well, there never seemed to be a good time."

Now Mom started tearing up. "Oh, Caroline! What were you up to?" She hugged the kid to her chest gently, and the kid squeezed back.

Then everything went blurry before clearing up again.

It was dark and wet. A sour-faced teenager was waiting outside a house.

And I knew why she was mad.

She'd snuck out to go to a party and her parents found out. Her mom had called to say she was on her way to pick her up. The party had just started, and the girl had argued with her about staying longer and catching a ride back with friends. But she'd been ordered to wait for her mother in the front of the house, on the sidewalk, and the girl was still fuming. All her friends had given her sympathetic looks as she muttered that she had to go.

Her mother's car pulled up and she got in, slamming the door.

Again, I was watching from afar, and I cringed inside. I turned away from the girl's bratty behavior, appalled, because I remembered this very night, the last night I saw my mother alive.

"Thanks a lot," the girl said, folding her arms across her chest.

My gaze was on a different car as I listened uncomfortably to the petulant voice.

Another car hummed at a distance from Mom's, its lights off. A woman sat behind the wheel, watching the teenager and her mother. She was familiar, but I couldn't place her. I saw her face as she listened to the girl—don't ask me how I knew she could hear from so far away, I just did. The woman's chin came down, her eyes narrowing, eyebrows drawn together in a menacing scowl. It was frightening. There was a growling sound, but I couldn't figure out where it came from. Both cars were heading down the street, and my senses floated above them. I was there in thought, but had no corporeal form. I recognized that this was a dream, yet it felt too real for me to watch without dreading the next few moments, knowing what was ahead, my heart pounding in sick anticipation.

Mom's car pulled up across the street from a newspaper machine. The news was old, but my mother was collecting newspapers for the class she was teaching tomorrow. Although she had long since stopped working in order to take care of me, she occasionally subbed for other teachers in the school district. I remembered that she was teaching sixth graders that week, and she was bringing newspapers for her unit on writing eyewitness articles.

She had no idea that she would be in them the next day.

A painful sob woke me. It was my sob. Here I was again, waking up crying. I prayed that I hadn't woken Dad. My door was still closed and I heard no sounds outside my door. *Thank you, God,* I thought.

It was a while before I fell asleep again; I kept seeing the strange woman's scowl and the deadly look in her eyes. But when I finally did sleep, it was dreamless.

12

MINIONS

"SO, THROW ME A bone, would you?" pleaded Ruthie. She was asking about Isaac, and about what had happened when she'd dropped me off after school yesterday. It was fun making her wait. She got so worked up. But I couldn't keep her in suspense any longer. The thing was, I just couldn't work up the excitement I had felt yesterday when Isaac asked me to the dance. Today, it was overshadowed by a sense of apprehension I didn't understand. Part of me wondered if I should have said no.

"Well, what if I said nothing happened?" I dragged it out a little longer.

Ruthie finally relented. "Well, I guess I read the situation differently," she mused. We were driving to school, and cutting it close to bell time. "My skills are seriously slacking. I could have sworn I saw some *situation manipulation* happening there in the backseat. Plus that whole kissing chase the other day. I mean, geez! And what was up with you two in the backseat, anyway? He's been hitting on you for days!"

"What?" Should I have figured that out? I wondered. "I thought Phoebe called *shotgun* again?"

"Oh, please! Shotgun? The guy's as big as Sasquatch! Phoebe would not have made him sit in the back if he didn't want to."

So much for being the smart kid in class. I sighed. "Well, what if I said your skills are right on?"

We were just pulling into the school parking lot. Ruthie gasped and whipped into a parking place so quickly I braced myself for impact. *Note to self: Don't surprise Ruthie while she's drivin.*

"What the freak is wrong with you!" she practically screamed at me, but with no real anger. She smiled smugly. "I knew it. Come on, give up the goods. Right now, or I'll keep you here until you do." The door locks clicked. I rolled my eyes. She was so over the top sometimes.

"Okay, okay. He asked me to Homecoming." The words rushed out of my mouth. "And I said yes. Now can we get to class? I don't want to be late!"

"Homecoming? Wow, that boy works fast. I should have seen it coming. I mean, dang, girl, you are fine this year, and the wolves were totally circling yesterday." I laughed, but she continued, "Isaac is a smart boy. Realized he'd have to jump on it to beat the others."

"Ha! Others! Whatever!" I smacked her on the shoulder. "Let's go!"

She unlocked the doors and we hurried off to class with her peppering me with comments like "So, how did he ask?" "You are so lucky!" "Val better ask me!" "We can go dress shopping together!" and on and on. But I wasn't into it

I was still freaking out inside about last night's dreams. They had felt so real, yet, of course, they couldn't be. And that woman's face haunted me. So familiar, but... Who was she? Or was she really someone at all? Could she be some random face from last year? Because, I didn't remember it very well at all. Was I finally losing my mind just when everything seemed to be getting better? All these thoughts flitted through my mind, and I barely heard Ruthie as she rattled on.

OUR LUNCH TABLE WAS crowded. Isaac, Phoebe, and Ruthie were the usuals. But now Val's football buddy, Jake, had joined us. Jake was so blatant in his attempts at flirting with Phoebe, I was ready to throw

up right then and there. If he said how beautiful she was one more time, I was going to join Bobby's table again. And if Zander showed up to join the Phoebe adoration club, I was really leaving.

Isaac seemed to share my sentiments. He was openly glaring at Jake, and I was afraid he was going to punch him or something if I didn't redirect his attention.

"Uh, Isaac, what exactly did you do this summer, anyway? Phoebe said something about camping, right?" Isaac turned to me. Bingo. Danger averted. Mission accomplished. But suddenly I was remembering my conversation with Ruthie before school. As I looked into his brown eyes, I thought, *He really is one of the most good-looking guys at our school. I can't believe he asked me to Homecoming.*

Isaac turned his back on the flirting across from us, leaning his side against the table, an elbow resting on its surface between us. I felt a little mesmerized, and a smile spread across my lips.

"Our family always goes camping deep in the forest, well away from any trails used by hu—uh, hikers. Do you like camping?" he asked.

"Well," I paused, "I don't know. My mom didn't like it, so we never went." I felt a hitch in my throat, remembering Mom. Isaac must have seen the pain flicker across my face, because he took up the conversation quickly.

"Yeah, we go a lot. Always have. We hit the beach, too. We just love this area, you know. So much of everything close by. Anyway, it's also a pretty cheap vacation, too, which my parents love." He laughed.

I wondered if Isaac's family worried about money. He didn't seem to be lacking anything. He and Phoebe didn't wear the most expensive brands, but their clothes always looked nice. Who was I kidding? They would look good in rags.

"It's more than I did this summer. We stayed home and I got a job at the recreation center," I said.

"Cool," he said. "What did you do there?"

"Sometimes I worked at the front desk. But most of the time I lifeguarded and helped with youth basketball."

"Wow! I didn't know you were a swimmer." He looked amazed. I thought I knew why. If most of his impression of me was based on last year, he must have thought I was a boring lump of clay. I looked down shyly at my lap.

"Yeah, I was on a swim team since I was a kid. Actually, I was in a lot of sports before, well, before..." I shrugged, my eyes still in my lap.

"I'm not surprised," said a familiar voice from the base of the maple tree. Somewhere during our lunch, Zander must have snuck in and staked out his old spot by the tree. "You look like an athlete to me," he continued.

Isaac growled slightly, and the entire lunch table paused to look over at Zander. Phoebe lit up like a Christmas tree.

A blush stole over my cheeks at his words. What did he mean? Did I look strong like an ox or fit like an aerobics instructor? Athletic like David Beckham or athletic like Anna Kournikova? I wasn't sure how to respond, so I just smiled hesitantly at him and said, "Hey. I saw you after school the other day. Who was that giving you a ride out of here?"

"Oh him. That was just my brother." So they were related. He pulled out an apple and took a bite. He always seemed to have an apple for lunch.

"Always an apple, huh?" I said, for lack of a smarter comment to make. I cringed inwardly at my poor attempt to make conversation. Seeing him again made my mind a little numb.

"You know what they say, apple a day…blah…blah…blah…"

"Tru has never been sick a day in her life," blurted Ruthie.

Now everyone looked at me. My face heated up again.

"Really?" scoffed Phoebe. "That would be pretty amazing. You probably don't remember being sick, though," she rationalized.

"Nope," said Ruthie. "I've known her almost my entire life, and she's never been sick—not even a cold. It's so not fair." My eyes were "shushing" her, but she just wasn't getting it. "She pretended to be sick a couple times, so we could skip school, but, yeah, pretty awesome."

Ruthie just didn't know when to stop.

Everyone was looking at me. I could almost hear what they were thinking: Weirdo! I couldn't believe my best friend had told everyone something so private—well, private to me. I understood that she didn't realize I hated that kind of attention. I knew she thought it was cool. But deep down inside I knew it was one more thing that set me apart from normal, like seeing in the dark. I knew I was overreacting, but I couldn't help it. I was so uncomfortable, I started to gather my things to leave. Only seconds had passed, but they felt like minutes to me—minutes of others staring at me like I was under a microscope.

Ruthie finally caught on to the fact that she had put her foot in her mouth. I could see it in her face. But what could she say now to fix it?

"You think that's cool?" Isaac's hands held me in place. "I won the hot dog eating contest in Santa Cruz this year."

"It's true," said Phoebe. "And my parents forced me to stay and watch. I think it's the first time he's ever been full!" She chimed with laughter. "Seriously, he could eat a horse!" Her eyes twinkled at Isaac, and something unsaid passed between them.

I settled back down as the attention moved away from me. Isaac's bragging had set off Val and Jake, who went off about food contests, how much they could eat, and even the grossest things they had consumed—clearly a popular guy topic. I sneaked a look at Zander. He was still looking at me, but he just smiled, not like I was weird, but more conspiratorially as he rolled his eyes at the guys' nonsensical bragging. The huge knot in my stomach finally started unraveling. Then I looked over at Ruthie. She met my gaze and mouthed the words "I'm sorry!" with a please-don't-hate-me look. I just pressed my lips together. I wasn't forgiving her quite yet, but I hadn't become the freak show that I expected.

AFTER THAT SCHOOL PASSED pleasantly and before I knew it, I was walking to English. As was the custom in many California schools, the classrooms opened to outdoor covered sidewalks, which spread like a web to all the other buildings scattered across campus. I was rounding the corner in a rush because the bell was about to ring when two girls sideswiped me going different directions. This spun me in a circle, sending my books flying, and I threw out my hands to stop my fall. I looked up to catch the mock surprise from my assailants—who just happened to be Zena groupies.

"Oh my gosh! I'm *sooo* sorry."

"You should really look where you're going! You could hurt someone."

Then they hurried off giggling, just as the bell sounded. I caught the words "psycho" and "brain damage." Gathering up my stuff, I noticed that my hands were bleeding. As I rubbed them on my pants, I saw a small tear across one knee, ruining one of my new pairs of jeans. A long sigh escaped me and I continued on to class. Maybe Mr. Mac wouldn't notice me sneaking in.

He was writing on the chalkboard as I walked quietly toward some empty seats in the back.

"Just getting here, Tru?" Zena's voice was loud and clear, and Mr. Mac turned from the board. Zena smirked. I closed my eyes in defeat.

"Ach, Ms. Parker. You know how I feel about being late, lass. I'm afraid that will have to be a tardy." He marked his attendance book with a reluctant look. I knew he was making a point for the whole class. I was probably the first tardy of the school year. It was way too soon to start collecting tardies. I had a feeling I would need some later.

By now, my hands were really stinging. I slipped into a seat and took a look at them. Deep and dirty scratches stretched across each palm, blood still oozing. There was nothing I could do for now, unless I asked to go see the nurse. But I didn't want to, especially in front of Zena. I knew she was responsible for this. I couldn't give her the satisfaction.

Gratefully, I acknowledged this was the last class of the day and I could go home and nurse my wounds in private. Mr. Mac cleared his throat and announced that he wanted everyone to pick a partner for our first project. He would give us a few minutes to exchange contact information and get to know each other a bit better—we were supposed to team up with someone we didn't know very well. Kids jumped out of their chairs, racing for their friends. Typical. I didn't feel like even trying, so I just laid my head on the desk, cradling my sore hands on my lap.

"Here, let me see them." Zander's voice drifted over from the empty desk next to me—at least it had been empty when I sat down. I lifted my head with a questioning look.

"See what?"

"Hands. I can tell there's something wrong with them."

So he had great powers of observation. Goodie for him. My life sucked.

I felt a hate laser stabbing at me from half the classroom away. I turned my head. Zena was the shooter. *Whatever*, I thought, not understanding what I had done to her this time.

Zander carefully picked up my hands and opened them. A warm hum enveloped my abused appendages. This time we didn't pull away. He brushed his fingertips across my palms. It didn't sting, but I was afraid it would and pressed my hands together again, sucking in my breath. He didn't force my hands apart. He just held them between his as waves of heat pulsed across my injuries. I didn't want him to let go. I felt like drowning in his endless, deep, sea-blue gaze.

"I kinda fell before class," I whispered hoarsely, hoping to prolong the contact.

"I thought athletic people weren't clumsy," he said, the corner of his mouth turned up. His thumbs rubbed against the backs of my hands.

"Yeah, well, I had some help falling." That's all I was going to say. No need to point fingers. I mean, what good would it do? The culprits were part of Zena's girl gang, which meant there would be no justice. And I really didn't want to sound like a whiner.

"Seriously?"

"Um, yeah, but if you think *I* look bad, you should see *them.*" I tried to joke.

He smiled. "Them? Seriously? What kind of school is this?"

I laughed weakly.

He grunted. "What did you do? Steal their lipstick?" His eyes crinkled at the corners.

"I know. Really. Military school would be too good for them."

"Girls are so weird," he smirked. "Why can't you just have a good clean fight and make up like us guys? You are so complicated."

"Hey, I'm with you!" I agreed. "I hate that stuff. It's not like I'm trying to be Miss Popular, anyway."

Inside, I cringed because that's exactly what I was doing this year with Ruthie's help.

"When someone else has something they want, they get jealous and strike out. That's usually why bullies do what they do."

"Ha! I don't have anything anyone else would want!" I rolled my eyes at his absurdity.

Suddenly his face was really close. "Oh yes you do." I forgot about Zena, Mr. Mac, and the rest of the chattering kids around me as we shared a long glance. Was that admiration in his eyes? My heart flip-flopped.

"I don't know what you're talking about," I whispered, breathlessly.

"Really?" he said doubtfully. "You do have mirrors in your house, right?" He gently let go of my hands and brushed a thick wave of hair from my eyes. I felt the lack of warmth around my hands like a coat removed in a blizzard, and shivered. At least that's the reason I told myself I shivered. I was still processing his subtle compliment. He reached for his backpack and rummaged in it until he came up with a small tube.

"You carry antibiotic ointment with you," I stated. "Very prepared. What are you? A Boy Scout?" I felt my lips curving up at one corner. Despite high school rivalries and my own numerous inadequacies, I felt happy.

He smiled. "I've been known to get into a few scrapes, myself, so I learned to be prepared. Here, let's see your hands again."

I laid them open, still drinking in his face. His eyebrows pushed together in perplexity, and I followed his gaze to my hands. The scratches were gone, the skin totally healed as if it had never been injured. Only the blood and dirt remained. I realized they didn't hurt anymore.

"What?" I gasped. We looked at each other, amazed. "I don't get it!" Was I losing it? "You saw them, right?"

Zander ran his hands over mine, turning them over and over.

"All right, class. Back to your seats," ordered Mr. Mac.

Zander and I pulled apart slowly. He looked warily at me and I wanted to beg him to believe me. I wondered what he was thinking and hoped he didn't think I was making it up, because I was just as mystified. If I didn't have dried blood and dirt smeared all over my hands, I would not have believed that they had ever been hurt. I pulled out my notebook and peeked at him next to me. He was turned forward, rubbing his face with his hands as if tired. He blinked his eyes a few times and then squished his eyebrows together in concentration. He looked confused, but no more than I did. I started to turn back and noticed him skillfully hiding a cell phone to one side, out of sight for most people. He was texting someone.

A shiver went up my spine. Something really miraculous had happened. My hands had healed or I was hallucinating. I felt like an idiot just thinking it. Did someone slip me something? Did I imagine it? No, Zander seemed just as confused.

Could Zander have caused it? I recalled the warmth of his hands as they held mine. Or did I do something? Did he think I had been lying about them? Great. Now I was a lying psycho.

When class ended, Zander walked me to the door. Again I felt Zena's hate laser. Again I ignored it.

"Tru," he said, "do you have time to, uh, talk today?"

"I don't know what happened, you know," I said defensively.

"Yeah, I got that." He paused as several students pushed their way past us, out of the classroom. "That was...weird, but I had some other questions for you."

Questions, I thought. Alarms were going off in my head. I doubted this was about homework, but...

"You mean about the assignment? We didn't get to talk, but did you want to partner up for the project?" I asked, a sliver of hope in my voice.

He hesitated, then said, "Yeah, I get the feeling you are one of the smart kids, and being your partner is definitely in my favor."

Oh great! Now I'm the nerd who helps the beautiful people with homework. I cringed inside.

"But that's not the only reason I want to be your partner." He leaned against the doorframe, looking down at me with a drool-worthy smile. I was totally unprepared for that kind of charm. So I said the first thing that came to my mind.

"Sure! When do you wanna start working on it?"

His smile widened. "Well, what about after school today? Say in an hour or so? I have something to take care of before I can meet you."

"Okay." The word was delivered in such a breathy and girly voice, I'm ashamed to admit it ever came out of my mouth. I cleared my throat and continued. "Where should we meet?"

"Can I come over to your place? I'm in an extended stay hotel until we find a house, so it's not very private."

When he said the word "hotel" and "private" in the same sentence, I almost choked. (What do you expect? I was a hormone-driven teenager, after all. And I watched way too much TV smut with Ruthie.) I wasn't sure where he was going with this line of thought. What was I doing? I hardly knew him.

I couldn't help blurting out, "My dad will probably be home, but it should be quiet enough. He spends most of his time working in the garage. He may come in and out a bit, but...uh...we should be able to...uh...study..." I was rambling. Did he get that I was emphasizing that I had a chaperone? Did he see that I was kind of freaking out about it? I felt like such a moron. He seemed to realize what I was thinking, and backtracked quickly.

"Oh, yeah, I didn't mean...well...I just...if you want to meet at the library instead, that's okay, too."

Alrighty, I thought. Talk about jumping to conclusions. He wasn't hitting on me—why would he be hitting on me? He liked Phoebe. All that "you're special" stuff was just him being a nice guy. I mentally smacked my head a few times. He really did want to work on the project. Fortunately, I loved Shakespeare and wouldn't embarrass myself. I could do this.

In a much calmer voice, I said, "No. That's okay. My place is easier since I don't drive yet."

I wrote down my address and phone number for him and said goodbye, happy that he seemed to have forgotten about that weird hand episode.

My heart fluttered nervously as I walked to my locker, where I knew Ruthie would be waiting. I was thinking about studying with Zander when I stopped suddenly. Wait a minute. What was I doing? Yesterday I agreed to go to Homecoming with Isaac, and just now I had agreed to meet with another boy in my home to work on our project. What was the protocol for this? If one went to Homecoming with someone, did that mean they were "exclusive," that they couldn't see another person even for homework? What did that mean, exactly? Would Isaac be offended? How did my life get so complicated?

All too soon, I arrived at my locker. The lunch gang was there, too. Val had his arm around my best friend. I gave him a sour look.

"What happened to you?" Ruthie demanded. Her fashionista senses had zeroed in on my ripped jeans. In the last five minutes I had forgotten my fall before class. Was there such a thing as temporary ADD?

"Zena's minions," I stated simply.

Isaac stepped up to examine me. "Are you hurt?" he asked.

I paled, not from pain but from acute guilt. He looked so concerned about me. If I were a good person, I would have thought about how he might feel before agreeing to meet with Zander. At least I should tell him. Maybe. No. He'd want to be there and then it would be Awkwardville again. Or was I just blowing this out of proportion? What did I know? I had never dealt with this sort of thing before. Ugh! This sucked!

"Just my pride," I replied with chagrin. "I also got to be Mr. Mac's poster child for tardies."

"Zena!" Ruthie muttered between clenched teeth, like it was something disgusting you stepped in on the sidewalk. Val seemed surprised.

Phoebe looked confused. "Zena Taylor pushed you down, and you got a tardy?"

"No, I got sideswiped by Juliana and Summer—Zena's minions. Then Zena made sure Mr. Mac noticed me sneaking into class late—seconds late, I might add. She's up to her old tricks again." I looked back to Ruthie. "She gave me the hate laser."

Val wailed dramatically, waving his hands. "Oh, not the hate laser!"

Ruthie smacked him in the shoulder. "Not cool, Val! You have no idea." She turned back to me sympathetically. "So, here we go again. I guess it's going to be one of those years...I thought she was going to move to L.A. or something."

"She wishes," I said.

"We wish," we both said together.

"I get the feeling she's done this sort of thing before?" asked Isaac. "Why doesn't she get into trouble?"

Phoebe answered, looking at Ruthie and me, "She's good at it, isn't she?"

"Zena, aka Cruella de Vil," said Ruthie.

Val piped in. "I don't get it. Because Cruella totally looks evil. Seriously, how did they not know she was the bad guy?" Everyone ignored him but Jake.

"Dude! I know, right? Disney villains are so obvious!"

I sighed. "She always gets her way—and I don't know how. It's like all the teachers are on her side. I never figured it out."

"Is this an ongoing feud? You and Ruthie against Queen of Evil and her sidekicks?" said Isaac.

"Pretty much," I answered. "She doesn't strike every year, at least not that often, but I have a feeling this year is her big comeback."

"Well," said Isaac, "this year you've got backup—us!"

Phoebe smiled alongside her brother. Val and Jake didn't seem to be taking the situation seriously, playfully punching each other, their conversation having already moved on to the upcoming football game.

"Well, vámanos, mis amigos!" Ruthie led the way to her car.

I got into the backseat with Isaac again while Ruthie said goodbye to Val and Jake. Phoebe chatted up Ruthie, which left Isaac asking about my day. I was a little too close to him to converse comfortably, especially now with the guilt lying heavily in my stomach like too much lasagna. I kept my comments short and concise. Plus, my mind was bouncing back to my disappearing hand injuries; so after enough one-word answers, he gave up and joined Phoebe and Ruthie's conversation. When Phoebe helped me out of the back, I thought I saw her sniff the air. There was no repeat bathroom request and I said goodbye, noting Isaac's slightly hurt gaze. More guilt.

"Dad!" I yelled as I opened the front door. There was no answer.

Then I remembered to turn my cell phone ringer back on. There was a strict no-cell-phone policy at school and Mr. Fuller, the Vice Principal, had a box full of confiscated phones sitting in a locked glass box you could see through the office window. It was a great tactic because every time I walked by it, I frantically checked to make sure my phone was turned off. There were no second chances, and it only took one phone ring near a faculty member to lose your phone.

Sure enough, there was a message from Dad. He had been called in to the office again, and he was going to be late returning home. Then I remembered that he said he'd be on location a lot this week. He probably wouldn't be home any time soon. *Perfect*, I thought apprehensively.

That made me a liar. Dad wouldn't be working in the garage while Zander and I studied. He wouldn't even be home. Awkward. I should cancel, I thought, because Dad would be angry if he came home and saw me alone with a boy. I knew that much. But I didn't have his phone number. I would just have to go with it and hope Dad didn't come until after Zander left.

13

MIND-WHAMMY

MIRACULOUSLY, I WAS ABLE to get most of my homework done before Zander showed up. It was 4:00 when I heard the doorbell. Nervously, I checked my appearance in the hall mirror before opening the door. I had switched my torn jeans and Converses for a pair of shorts and flip-flops. Very casual, but it was a warm day and we didn't have air conditioning.

Zander wore the same clothes that I'd seen him in at school—a wrecked pair of jeans, a band T-shirt, and Vans. His dark chestnut hair looked a little windblown, but it just made him look like he had stepped off a modeling shoot where they have all the fans blowing to make you look sexier. Yeah, it worked for him.

"Can I come in?" he asked after I stood there dumbly.

After a mental self-smack, I pulled myself together. "Yeah, come on in." I gestured toward the kitchen area. "You want to study at the kitchen table?"

"Sure." He swung his backpack off his shoulder as he headed inside. He took in the whole place with a sweeping glance. It was an outdated one-story home still sporting Mom's feminine style, but everything looked a bit threadbare. Mom talked about updating for years, and it just never happened. But she always kept it clean and organized, two things that were sort of missing these days. And Dad always said he liked it "original," meaning he didn't want to replace anything. I was not as good at cleaning as Mom, and Dad didn't realize that it needed to be cleaned most of the time. I was grateful he liked to cook, although he often left the kitchen a mess. I had tidied up when I got home, but suddenly noticed the dust everywhere. I forgot to dust! I was gaining a newfound respect for my mother all the time, because it was never dusty before and I seriously didn't remember her dusting.

I may have forgotten the dusting, but Mom's hospitality lessons kicked in, and I couldn't sit down without offering Zander something to drink. So, with two sodas we settled at the table.

"Thanks again, Tru, for being my partner. Shakespeare is kind of hard to understand, at least I think so," said Zander, smiling. He pulled out our textbook.

That's when I really knew he was here for the studying, nothing else, because he was jumping right into the schoolwork. In one respect, I was glad. No pressure and less guilt over Isaac. But on the other hand, I felt a little miffed at myself for hoping for more. I was seriously screwed up.

"That's okay. It's a group project, so we're supposed to work on it together anyway. It will probably get easier as we read it."

Twenty minutes later, I reassessed him. After all of his complaining, he had picked it up faster than I expected. His comments were pretty astute, like he had read this before. I eyed him suspiciously.

"A little young to fall in love, wouldn't you say?" asked Zander sardonically.

I shrugged off my skepticism. "Yeah." I laughed. "My biggest challenge at thirteen was how Ruthie and I were going to convince our parents to let us go to a concert in Santa Cruz," I answered.

"You're lucky you got to go," he smiled, "assuming you did."

"Yeah. Ruthie's parents are really overprotective, but Ruthie has amazing manipulation skills. She became the model daughter for two weeks before she asked them. She caught them off guard."

"Ha!" he snorted. "I can see that. She seems pretty crafty. How did you convince your parents?"

"Oh, I got to go, but only if they came, too," I said with chagrin.

Zander hooted. “Sounds like fun.”

“Hmm. It was okay.” I twirled my pencil absently. “So, what was your favorite concert?” I asked.

“Actually, I’ve never been to a concert,” he admitted. “That’s why I said you are lucky.”

“Wow! You’re kidding, right?”

“No, really. My father doesn’t approve of concerts—thinks they are a waste of time—I should make better use of my time, yada yada yada.”

I looked at him thoughtfully, wondering about his childhood. Sounded like a strict household to me. Zander noticed me staring and cleared his throat. I blushed.

“So,” he said, “back to medieval teenagers falling in love… Yay…” He didn’t seem impressed by the epic love story.

I felt I needed to defend the young couple. “You know, back then, their life expectancy was pretty low. So if people only lived to be thirty or forty, then Juliet was considered an adult, almost middle-aged. Perhaps they were just making the most of their short lives.”

“I guess you’re right,” he consented. “Don’t they say that you’re only as old as you think you are?” He gazed absently out the kitchen window. “Sometimes I feel ancient.”

“Or, you can live several years in just a few months,” I countered. Last year I had grown up in a moment—when my mother died in front of me. I didn't know if I'd ever be that carefree girl again, which was good in some ways.

Zander swung his gaze over to me sympathetically. "I heard you lost your mother last year," he said softly.

I bet that wasn't all he heard. "I suppose you heard that I kind of lost it, too." I kept my eyes on our textbook, afraid to see the pity, and maybe the disgust.

But I didn't feel pity from him, like I did from everyone else. I wondered at that. I finally glanced up. He was staring down at me.

"People who like to talk about that haven't been through what you went through."

I blinked back the moisture that suddenly gathered in my eyes. Clearing my throat, I asked, "What about your parents? Do you live with them?"

"Yeah, but we don't really get along, at least my father and I don't," he said. "Mother's okay, but she always sides with Father." He looked away uncomfortably.

He may not have lost a parent, but he understood pain. I could see it in his eyes, and suddenly I wanted to take away the pain, whatever it was. My hand automatically reached to cover his, but he pulled away. My face flushed in embarrassment, and I watched him get up from the table and walk quickly over to the kitchen window.

Oh man, I thought, *I'm such an idiot.* What was I doing?

"Tru, do you have a dog?" he asked.

What was with that? Then I remembered the paw prints in the backyard.

"No, but I saw some paw prints out there yesterday. Maybe a neighbor's dog is getting in. Why, do you see one?" I got up to look out the window. Something big and furry was leaping over our back fence, into another yard. Zander ran out the back door in a flash. Before I could follow him, I saw him pursue another giant furball over the fence. My thoughts went back to the wolf I had seen my first day of school. No, it wasn't possible! Whatever it was, I was pretty sure Zander shouldn't be chasing it.

Without giving it a thought, I grabbed a knife from the butcher block and headed out the back door. I walked warily around the side of the house to check if the gate was open. It was closed. I stepped cautiously to the other side of the house, a covered area where we kept our trash cans. The knife was trembling in my hand, but I moved forward anyway. Nothing. Where had he gone?

"Zander!" I called out, my voice cracking. A growl vibrated through the air, behind me, behind our fence. Something was on the other side. I knew the Jenkins didn't have a dog and automatically backed away.

"Tru! Look out!" Zander was leaping toward me over our fence. That alone was confusing, because our fence was hecka tall, and I don't think even our school's track team could leap that high. Bewildered, I twisted around too quickly and tripped over a hose.

"Aagh!" I felt the blade sink into my arm, which had to be one of the strangest sensations I've ever felt. I lay there crumpled on the ground, the steel of the knife sticking out of my left arm, below my elbow. I sat up because there were now two Jurassic-sized furballs in my backyard, and Zander was facing them both.

They were two of the largest wolves I'd ever seen, standing maybe four feet tall, on all four paws. The wolves I'd seen in the zoo were definitely smaller. The fur on these wolves was raised in bunches, not a happy stance. One looked like the animal Ruthie and I had seen the first day of school. It had dark brown fur with gold streaks along its sides. The other wolf sported gray fur with black streaks. And they both snarled ominously at Zander. We had to get out of here.

Biting my lip, I pulled the blade out of my arm. The pain was excruciating, the sensation sickening, and blood immediately poured from the wound. A ragged and unstoppable whimper erupted from my mouth. I held my arm to my side tightly, biting my lips closed and wrapping the lower part of my shirt around my bleeding limb.

"Tru!" Zander headed toward me, staring at my arm. But the brown wolf darted in front of him and snapped its jaws with a growl. He was trapped between them. The gray one didn't seem to know what to do. It kept moving its head from me to Zander and to the other wolf. We were all suspended, waiting for someone to make a move.

"Don't move, Tru," ordered Zander. No worries, I wasn't going anywhere. Slowly the brown wolf backed toward me. Zander looked frantic, but he was going to be dog food if he moved an inch.

The brown wolf turned slightly as it backed up and ended up with all of us in its sights. I could see directly into its golden eyes. They looked into mine, *right into me*, like it knew me, like it was trying to tell me something. Suddenly, I wasn't scared anymore. The wolf seemed to urge me to trust it, stretching out its nose toward me, ever so slowly. A warning growl came from the other wolf, but I ignored it and met the nose coming toward me with my palm out.

"Don't, Tru!" Zander's desperate plea flowed over me, but I disregarded him, too.

The tip of a warm tongue lapped at my fingers, spreading warmth up my arm and throughout my whole body. It reminded me of something, but I couldn't place the feeling. It was so good, so comforting. I reached further and rubbed my fingers through its fur along the jaw. A rumble ran through the wolf, and something between a laugh and a sob welled up in me. I knew this wolf, but from where I couldn't remember. It licked my injured arm, nudging away the material and lapping at the wound. It didn't hurt at all, and I looked up at Zander in amazement.

He looked just as shocked as I did. The gray wolf still stood between us, its stance protective. I didn't understand any of this. Suddenly, my wolf (in those few moments, that's how I had begun to think of it) faltered, dropping its head in my lap. The gray one growled again, moving closer, menacingly. Without hesitation, I ran my hand over the forehead of the beautiful animal in my lap, frantic that it was hurt. This moment seemed strangely familiar, and I desperately wanted this wolf to be well.

"No, no! Please be okay. I can't lose you, too!" I pressed my face into its warm fur. It felt so good. "Please," I urged. A soft glow outlined the wolf, its fur swaying to an unknown breeze. And then its eyelids lifted and its jaw widened.

Tears of happiness trickled down my cheeks as I darted a quick smile over to Zander. But Zander was reaching inside his waistband, causing the gray wolf to leap toward him.

This snapped my wolf out of its weakened state. Moving like a blur, it leaped toward the gray wolf just as a shot rang out, followed by a painful whine. The gray went down, but only for a second. It was bleeding, but the injury wasn't stopping him. Zander had some kind of gun in his hand and was preparing to shoot again. However, now both wolves were coming at him, from opposite sides.

"No!" I yelled at him. It just seemed wrong to hurt these creatures. I jumped up and was at his side in a second, pulling down his arm. My wolf immediately blocked the gray one, who snapped back at it. Just then, tires screeched to a stop in the street and a car door slammed. Running feet headed toward the gate.

The two wolves growled, their heads lowering. Zander's brother burst through the entrance. In a move that looked practiced, both wolves circled us in opposite directions, bounded onto the garbage cans against the back of the fence, and disappeared into the next yard.

Zander's brother continued into the backyard until he loomed over us, a gun in his hand.

"What happened?" he barked. Not "what was that?" or "are you all right?" or even "did you get the license plate number?" He seemed remarkably calm for the situation. When he looked around at me, he did a double-take.

"What are you doing here?" G.I. Joe brother gasped at me, his eyes softening.

Zander scoffed and rolled his eyes. "She lives here, doofus. This is Tru, the one I told you about," he said, turning to check out my arm. His brother pulled himself together with a shake, still peering at me warily.

"About time you got here," Zander threw at his brother angrily. "I thought you were supposed to be just around the corner!"

"I was. And you seem to be just fine."

"Yeah, I'm okay, but Tru's not. Here, let me see that." Zander turned my arm over while I scowled at their confusing conversation. I had completely forgotten about my knife wound. In fact, my arm didn't hurt anymore. I allowed him to examine it. He ran his fingers over the wound area. Streaks of blood were still drying, and the cut had closed up, just a puckered line remaining.

"Huh? Again?" I gasped. Zander's forehead was creased in perplexity. "What's going on?" I asked. "You saw it, didn't you? It was bleeding just a second ago!" I dropped down to the grass, holding my arm. "What's happening to me?" I said quietly to myself. But they both heard me.

"I'm not sure. But you seemed to know that wolf."

"Are you kidding me? I didn't know wolves got that big!"

Zander stared dubiously at me for a moment and then threw up his arms before walking over to his brother, who was climbing a ladder he'd found at the side of the house, to peer over the fence.

Zander paced back and forth furiously, telling his brother what had happened. I followed his movements, stunned by the developments of the past—how long had it been? Seconds, minutes, hours? It was a slice out of time, out of reality. Like a dream.

"You know what I have to do," his brother stated, stepping down from the fence.

Zander stopped in front of his brother, placing a hand on his shoulder. "No. It doesn't always work right. You could hurt her."

"Zander, if she's human, she can't know about this stuff. If she's idimmu, well, it won't matter anyway..." He drifted off, running a hand through his blond hair.

Okay, I might have been in shock, but I was not stupid. Two giant-sized wolves had really been in my backyard. Zander could leap over tall fences like a freaking superhero. My arm had just healed itself. And big brother didn't know if I was human or something else, *and* he wanted to do something to me that Zander didn't want him to do, which, by the way, might hurt me. I did what most logical people would do in this situation—I ran. My plan: Lock myself inside, dial 911, have a panic attack.

I made it inside the house, but a boot stopped the door from closing. I looked up from the black obstruction and into his face. Dark brown eyes glared at me, as if I were the one trying to break into his house and do God-only-knows-what to him. He squinted fiercely at me. It knocked me back—no, he hadn't touched me, but my head suddenly slammed with pain. I fell backward on the kitchen floor, grabbing my head and moaning.

"Stop it, Peter! Damn it! Stop it. Now!"

I barely made out Zander leaning over me, the pain blurring my vision. It felt like a knife was stabbing into my brain, like my eyes were bleeding and rolling into the back of their sockets. Suddenly all I could see was blackness, but I heard a scuffle and glass breaking before I passed out.

14

Reality Shift

I DON'T THINK I was unconscious for more than a few seconds, because Zander and his brother were still in my kitchen, and they were arguing pretty loudly. I remember seeing a similar situation on TV—some wildlife show about armadillos. Basically, play dead and the bad guy will leave; play dead and maybe I'd find out what was really going on.

"What part of *NO* did you not hear!" yelled Zander. Something large thumped roughly against the cupboards. I hoped it was G.I. Joe's head. Whatever he had done to me, well, I was still feeling the aftershocks, like little bolts of electricity through my brain. I wanted to hold my head between my hands, but I didn't want to move and gain their attention.

"Stand down, Zander!" his brother ordered. "This is protocol! We don't leave witnesses. Ever. What's with you?"

"You could have killed her, you idiot! And she may be more than we think!"

"She's fine, man, I promise. Back off, would you?"

A pause. It was so tempting to look, but I kept my eyes shut.

Finally, Zander spit out, "Fine! But how do you know she's okay?"

"Just check her pulse, Sherlock."

Warm fingers pressed against my neck. I panicked for a second, and I prayed that I wouldn't give myself away with a frantic pulse. The hum between us sent me warm waves and soothed my headache.

"She's okay," sighed Zander. "I'm going to move her to the couch in the other room." Strong arms lifted me and I felt weightless for a few seconds before being pressed against the couch cushions. A gentle hand brushed the hair out of my face.

"Now what do we do?" asked Zander.

"*We* don't do anything. You shouldn't even be here. You are going to be in enough trouble as it is."

"Then don't tell them."

A frustrated sigh.

"But if we find Dubois, we'll be forgiven anything," said Zander. "First things first. What happens with Tru now?"

"She shouldn't remember what happened here."

"Okay. Is she going to remember we had a study date today?"

My heart leapt at the word "date." He *had* considered it a date! My stomach fluttered in response. What was I thinking? First of all, had I forgotten Isaac? And second of all, something weird was happening, and I could not afford to be distracted by a "study date" or a cute boy—scratch that—make that a mysterious, gorgeous boy who carries a gun in his pocket and has a brute for a brother. I had to figure things out, and I'd play along with whatever story they required for now.

"Date, huh?"

"Uh, no, man! It's not like that! It's my cover!" defended Zander.

My blood began to boil. *Jerk*, I thought.

"Okay. But you have to stay focused," admonished his brother. "I think Father is right. You are still too young for this stuff."

"You know I'm not." Zander sounded like he was gritting his teeth.

"Whatever. She probably won't remember, but I'm not sure. It happened really fast and you messed up my concentration when you started beating on me. Seriously! What is wrong with you?"

"You deserved it. And she better not have permanent damage," Zander growled.

"Stow it, Zander."

Another pause.

"Fine. So who were the usemi? You think the brown one looked like Dubois?"

"Possibly. Looked like her description. Dad never let me be around when she went furry, so I don't know for sure. I have no idea who the other one is." He sighed with frustration.

"What did you learn from your *study date*?" he almost sneered.

"Nothing. We were reading here at the table. I was hoping to get some clue about what's up with her, and suddenly I saw the brown one in the backyard. I went to the window to get a better look and noticed it take off over the fence followed by the gray one. So I went after them."

I could hear Zander pacing beside the couch.

"You took off after two usemi in front of her?" Zander's brother sounded furious. But it didn't seem to faze Zander.

"Tru mentioned that she'd seen animal tracks in her backyard. This wasn't the first time they've been here."

"Why would they come here? What's the connection?" mused his brother. "What do you know about this girl? Is it possible she knows them?"

"I don't know."

"You've been in that school for days! Something is definitely going on there."

Footsteps paced back and forth beside the couch. Must be Zander.

"Hey, back there in the yard, you acted like you knew her. What was that about?" asked Zander.

"Nothing. She just reminded me of someone in Eden, one of Father's, you know... At first I really thought it was her. They look a lot alike, that's all. Anyway, I'm just wondering if there's a connection between the two."

"Who are you talking about? I've never seen anyone who looks like her." Zander's pacing had stopped.

"Some idimmu Dad has in the lower levels. I forgot you don't have clearance." I could hear the scorn in his voice. "Anyway, she's one of his special projects."

"Tru lives here with her father. Her mother is the one who died last year in that car accident Father was so excited about," said Zander.

At this point, I wondered if I had fallen asleep. Maybe I was dreaming, because this had all the characteristics of a nightmare. With the hand wedged between the couch and me, I pinched myself. No, not dreaming. Zander and his brother were still discussing strange creatures like they were real. I had watched plenty of supernatural movies—what teenager didn't—and I could put two and two together as well as the next person. They were talking about werewolves. But that was just silly. Yet, how else could I explain those wolves in my backyard?

"We know Dubois was here last year." Zander's brother was talking, his voice slightly higher. "They tracked her to this area and then found her prints all over that hit and run. Then the trail headed out of California and went cold. Any usemi or akharu living locally? I need to check the database again. We need to find the connection here."

Their conversation faded. I had stopped listening after *hit and run.* Were they talking about my mother? Was it possible that these guys knew who killed her? No. It was a hit and run, and the police had never found the driver. The car had been stolen, ditched a block away from the accident. It took all my self-control not to jump up and scream at them to tell me *who.* Who was this *Dubois*? They were talking about these usemi like they were people. Who were these guys? And what exactly were they?

The back door opened.

"Wait!" said Zander. "What am I supposed to tell Tru?"

"Nothing. Come with me for now and see what she remembers tomorrow."

I could hear Zander gathering up his books and stuffing them into his backpack. How could he just leave after what happened? *What a jerk,* I thought. The back door shut. A minute later, they drove away.

I could finally open my eyes. What was I supposed to think? What should I say to Zander tomorrow? Or should I call him tonight? I had no idea what to do. Dad could be coming home soon, but I definitely didn't want to discuss this with him.

Ruthie. She always knew what to do. Cradling my head, I got up to rummage through my backpack for my phone.

"Ruthie. I really need to talk to you."

"Yeah, I'm listening, girl," she responded. Suddenly she screamed, "Get out of here, you little freaks!" I held the phone away from my ear, wincing. "Oh, crap, girl, I didn't mean you. The raptors were circling again."

Her little brothers were constantly terrorizing her. There was nothing more tempting to two curious little boys as a closed door. Personally, I thought they tried to wind her up just to hear her scream. I swear she could almost shatter glass.

"Ruthie, I need to talk to you face-to-face," I insisted. "Can you come over now?"

"What time is it? Umm... It's almost dinnertime. Mom won't go for it."

"Tell her my dad isn't home and I need a friend. Tell her I need help with homework. Tell her I tried to dye my hair and messed up royally. Whatever it takes!"

"Geez, Tru!" Her voice was gentle. "Okay, she'll never believe the homework one. The hair dye one would work too well—she'd want to come over and help. No, let's go with option number one. I'm one hell of a good friend, right?"

I almost sobbed with relief. "Yes, Ruthie. You are the best!"

"I'll be right over."

15
CRAZY

"SO," MUSED MY BEST friend, "to sum it all up, you saw two wolves in your backyard that didn't attack you. You stabbed yourself with a knife, and Zander's brother did some hocus pocus on your brain to wipe your memory, but somehow it didn't work."

The way she said it, I wouldn't have believed it either. But I knew it happened. I was tempted to call Zander to confirm, but he didn't want me to remember, so what was the point? He'd play stupid even if it were the truth.

"Yeah..." my friend drawled. "Zander would be the hot guy you are not going to Homecoming with because another hot guy already asked you." She sighed dramatically. "You are so awesome!"

Ruthie and I were sitting on my bed. I had every window and door locked up tight. And Dad was still not home. I had explained most of it to her—I may have left out the magic healing of my hands at school and the fact that I had felt "connected" to the wolf, but I'd given her more than the overall picture.

"You don't believe me," I stated.

"Tru," she started.

"No, look at my arm!" I held it out. There was still dried blood on it, and a faint red line remained where the knife had stuck me.

She puzzled over it for a second. "Tru, wounds don't instantly heal." She sighed. "I have to say, girl, you're my best friend, but this is just too crazy."

Crazy. With my history, no wonder she doubted me. I probably would, too. Then I remembered the knife. It must still be outside. I grabbed her arm, pulling her off the bed and down the hall to the back door.

"I think I have proof!"

"Okay, okay! You don't have to drag me!"

"Oh, sorry." I stopped at the door and ran my hand through my hair. "It's just that I know you think I'm nuts, and I'm beginning to feel like I really am losing it. But I think the knife is still out in the backyard."

Ruthie heaved another long sigh. "All right, at least you aren't comatose. And honestly, this is pretty imaginative, I must say!"

I cringed. Yes, last year did seem like I'd been in a coma. I opened the door and led her outside. Just as I had hoped, there was the kitchen knife lying in the grass. It was covered in dried blood.

"No way!" Ruthie looked horrified as I picked it up and showed her. Real horror, not the supportive pretend stuff I'd been getting up until now.

"What's happening, Ruthie?" I asked, desperately. I looked across the grass at the garden area. "Come here," I said. "Maybe the footprints are still there."

We hustled over and sure enough there were lots of paw prints, too large for an average dog, and they overlapped each other like they had crossed this area multiple times. It made sense because this was near the area of fence they had crossed over.

"So," said Ruthie, her eyes wide with fear. "You said they went over the fence. Did you see what's on the other side?"

"No, not yet. But I'm going to." I handed her the knife and walked determinedly to the ladder Zander's brother had left near the fence line.

"What do you see?" asked Ruthie when I had climbed to the top of the fence.

What I saw was a mess. Our neighbors, Mr. and Mrs. Jenkins, were workaholics. They were gone from sunup to late every night. They had never bothered to landscape the backyard, and the already sad-looking grass had been overcome with weeds ages ago. Dirt patches appeared in various places. It looked like they might have used the covered patio in the past because a table sat unused in the center with a covered barbeque tucked under the kitchen window. A section of the back fence bordered the woods where a small creek ran. That must be where the wolves had entered. Our yard backed up against another neighbor's yard—we were entirely surrounded by neighbors. I looked more closely at the dirt patches. And even though the light was getting dim, I could see the evidence of the wolves—the same tracks were here, and they ran up to the back fence by the woods.

"It doesn't look like the Jenkins ever go in their backyard. I can see some of the same-looking footprints. I think they came in through the woods at the back of their yard."

"Holy cow, girl!" she exclaimed. "Wait one fried fish minute! Was it that dog we saw the first day of school?" She was finally putting the pieces together and taking this seriously. I climbed down the ladder and began putting it away. She followed close behind me, looking warily back at the fence.

"Yeah. The one that licked my arm looked like the one we saw that morning."

"What? It licked your arm?" She was in my face the second I turned around. "You didn't tell me that part!" Her voice was growing kind of loud. And I was feeling anxious being outside. It was getting darker, due to the fog rolling in. A long howl ripped through the night. It came from the woods. Ruthie and I quickly started backing toward the house.

"Come on. Let's go back in," I said, holding her arm. We turned and raced back to the house. Just as we got to the door, something slammed into the back fence. We heard some rustling and a very low growl. We weren't waiting around to investigate. With shaking hands, we locked ourselves in the house again. Ruthie stood a few feet from the door, her eyes wide as saucers.

Her voice wobbled as she said, "Was that what I think it was?"

I was shaking, too, and moved toward the sink to wash the knife.

"Yeah, I think so," I mumbled. I finished up and put the blade away. "Do you think I'm going insane?" I wasn't a fool. What I had told her could put me in the mental institute for real.

"Are you kidding?" she gasped. "If you are, then get me a matching straitjacket!"

Moments later, we sat cross-legged on my bed. I ran my hand over the patchwork quilt that my mom made for me when I was twelve. It was soft from so many washings. My parents upgraded my bed to a queen on my twelfth birthday so I would have room for Ruthie to sleep over. It had made me feel so much older. But right now I felt really young. Of all the crazy memories in this room, lots of giggles, lots of tears, lots of secrets—this topped them all. I could feel my life shifting in an irreversible way, but toward what exactly I didn't know.

Despite her lunch table revelation regarding my incredible health, I knew I could trust Ruthie with my biggest secrets, like my night vision. As children we explained it away as a secret superpower. As we got older, we decided it was just a fluke gift of nature and we should keep it to ourselves in case scientists decided to experiment on me—well, you never know.

I looked at Ruthie. She had calmed down since we came in the house. She'd always been so strong, dramatic, but never one for depression dives. She'd never deserted me when I lost it, and I knew that once she had it organized in her head, she would be back to her own awesomeness. She was deep-thinking, tapping her fingers on her knee and staring at my quilt.

"Okay," she said, pulling out of her trance. "So, your arm healed when the wolf licked you, huh?"

"Yeah, I guess so."

"Magical spit. That's awesome."

I laughed at her conclusion.

"Well," she said, "what else could it be?"

"Maybe it can heal stuff," I contended. "The wolf, I mean."

"Then why lick you? Come on, Tru! We've just passed into the Twilight Zone. Then there's Zander's brother, the freak of nature, who did some mumbo-jumbo mind thingie on you."

"Yeah, " I said, drawing it out because I wasn't sure how to explain it.

"Well, what's with that, anyway? I think we need to start over. There must be more that you aren't telling me."

I made a face again.

"Yeah, but it's even weirder." I hesitated.

"Weirder than wolves, magic healing, and psychic brothers?" she scoffed. She looked intensely at me for a second. My eyes started to tear up.

"Tru, what's going on?" she whispered and took my hand, squeezing it. I knew I had to tell her *everything*. Saying it out loud might help me not feel delusional. Besides, no one else would believe me. I squeezed her hand back.

I started with the first time I met Zander, at our lunch table. I told her about our "connection." I told her it had happened several times. And then I described how my hands had healed in class.

"Wait, stop right there," demanded Ruthie. "You feel a vibration when you touch him?" Of course she would focus on that, not the magical healing. "That is a seriously epic reaction, you know, right?"

We had both scooted up against my wall at the head of the bed.

"I know, right?" I mumbled. "I thought it was really cool, too, but now everything is so crazy. I mean, geez, he and his brother are some—uh—top secret agents, or something, chasing—uh—supernatural criminals, or whatever."

"They seem a little whacked to me, no offense," she offered, perhaps to cheer me up, because, really there didn't seem to be a happy ending to it.

I looked up at the ceiling, exasperated. "I know. But then, what if they aren't. Ruthie, those wolves were not ordinary. That one I told you about—I don't know—I could swear its eyes were human, like it knew me or liked me or, geez, I don't know! This is so weird! I feel like I'm in some kind of strange sci-fi movie or nightmare!"

"Here! I'll pinch you," she offered.

"Too late," I sighed. "I already tried it—"

I sat up quickly. "Wait! I totally forgot about the dreams!"

Ruthie grabbed my arm excitedly. "No way! You dreamed about him before he came, didn't you! Good Gravy, that's so romantic!"

"No, not him. I saw the wolf! Remember the first day of school and I said I'd dreamed about a wolf?"

"Oh yeah! Oooh, that's so weird!"

"Well, I've been having weird dreams since before the accident."

"What? Tru, I never knew! Like what?"

"If you recall, I was borderline psychotic last year, and Dad's been threatening to make me see a doctor."

"No way! A shrink?" She recoiled, her eyes bugging.

I slid off the bed to pace the room. "That's what I thought you'd say, and that's why I never told you, and everyone else would think even worse!"

She had the grace to look ashamed. "Sorry, Tru, just a reflex, that's all. You know I have an uncle in the mental hospital, and I'm seriously creeped out when Mom makes us visit him at Christmas."

"Yeah, yeah. Well, *talking* to a psychiatrist is not the same as being *committed* to a mental hospital! Even so, my dad thinks I'm having nightmares about the accident."

"Nobody would be surprised if you did. So, what are they about then?" she asked.

I pulled out my desk chair and straddled it backward.

"It's all really weird. Sometimes it's about this man killing his brother and the dead brother's wife finding him—and they're dressed in animal skins like, I don't know, cave people wore. Sometimes I'm in this smoky forest and I can hear someone calling my name, but it's not my name, yet I know it's me, and I can hear this kid crying her eyes out. Then this dog comes up to me and I'm so happy, but when it gets really close with its big teeth, I realize it's a wolf and I wake up—"

"Whoa, whoa, whoa!" interjected Ruthie. "Did you say *wolf?*"

"Yeah, that's the dream I had the night before school started."

"Okay, I'm so freaking out here." Ruthie was on her knees on the bed. Then she took a couple of deep breaths and sat back down. She gave me a nod to continue.

"So what else are you dreaming about?" she asked.

I heaved a big sigh and scrunched up my forehead in concentration.

"Well, I had a couple new ones last night. It really weirded me out because this time they were finally about my mom."

"Okay," prompted Ruthie.

"When I'm having these dreams, sometimes I *know* more than I *see*, if that makes sense."

"Huh?"

"For instance, this time I dreamed about Mom and Dad and Uncle Ira. My uncle was introducing a little girl to my parents."

"That doesn't seem very strange."

"The little girl was me," I stated pointedly.

"Oh, yeah, that's weird," she agreed. "Well, what happened in the dream?"

"It was like my parents were just meeting me for the first time, and Mom was saying how much I looked like her."

Ruthie kept interjecting, to urge me on as I paused now and then.

"My parents were looking at me like I was their favorite candy, you know, and Mom was saying something about Caroline, um, like she wondered what she had done. Like it had something to do with me."

"Who's Caroline?" asked Ruthie. By now she was on the edge of the bed across from me.

"I'm not sure, but I know Mom had a sister named Caroline. She died before I was born—at least that's what she always said."

"This is better than *Court of Palms*, I swear!"

"Unfortunately, this is my life!" I shot her a glare.

"Okay, okay. Sorry. It's just so gripping! Oscar-winning, I swear! What did your uncle do?"

"Oh yeah. Um. That was really weird—well, even weirder, I guess. He said that Caroline always wished we could meet—meaning Mom and me. How cracked is that?"

"Shank steak! It's so screwed up! No, give me a minute. I watch all sorts of screwed-up shows. I can put this together." Now she scooted off the bed to pace.

Suddenly her cell phone rang. We both jumped and screamed, but just a little. Then we laughed hysterically even though we weren't feeling humorous. Nerves.

"It's my mom. What time is it? Oh my gravy, it's 9:00!" She quickly answered her phone.

"Sorry, Mom. I wasn't watching the time. Yeah, I'm heading home right now." Pause. "Yes, I'm walking out the door." Pause. "Okay, okay. See you in a few!" She hung up.

"I know," I said. "You've got to go."

"Where's your dad, Tru?"

"He had to work late, I guess, but he should be home any minute. Don't worry. I'll be fine. For some reason, I don't feel like I have to worry about those wolves or whatever they were." I hugged her. "You are such a great friend, Ruthie!"

"I didn't get to analyze your dreams yet!" she complained.

I laughed, some of the tension leaving me. "Another day, another session, Doctor!" She laughed with me.

Suddenly we both heard the garage door opening. I peeked out my bedroom window to see my dad's truck pulling in.

"Shoot!" I said. "Dad's home. You better go fast!" Now we were giggling like old times.

"I'm out of here." Ruthie was through the front door before Dad made it into the house. Even though I'd told Ruthie I was fine with her leaving, I felt relieved that Dad was finally home.

Somehow, talking it all over with Ruthie made everything seem like it wasn't happening to me, like it was some show we had seen together. I was able to greet Dad like I'd had a completely normal day. Was it so bad that I was hiding it all from him?

16

VAMPIRES AND WEREWOLVES

THE NEXT MORNING, I was so nervous, I got clumsy, and Dad was giving me odd looks over breakfast. I deflected most of his questions by asking about his work—he loved to talk about the latest techno-gadget. But it wasn't working as well as normal. He knew something was up, so I hurried through my Cheerios and dashed back to brush my teeth before Ruthie showed up.

I dropped a perfunctory kiss on Dad's cheek and ran out the door just as she was pulling up.

"Hey there," Ruthie said. "I see you survived the night. Anything else happen?" She looked at me expectantly.

I eyed her carefully. She looked hopped up on caffeine. "Are you okay?" I asked.

"Yeah, yeah. I didn't sleep so well, maybe. Just going over everything in my mind. Had a hard time waking up, so I downed some of my dad's emergency energy drinks."

"As in plural?" Oh man.

"Yeah, yeah." She waved away my concern. "So what else happened?"

"Well, not much, not really. No unexpected visitors, if that's what you mean." I looked more closely at her. Her skin looked a little pale, her eyes big and wide. "Why? Anything happen to you?" Perhaps I shouldn't have told her about last night. Now she was scared, too, and dipping into Red Bull.

"I don't know. It was just weird. The whole time I drove home, I felt strange, like someone was watching me. I think I was just paranoid. And I could have sworn I saw a wolf along the side of the road on my way here this morning." She gripped the steering wheel until her knuckles turned white.

"Oh Ruthie. I'm sorry! I shouldn't have gotten you involved." My stomach clenched in regret. But she just shrugged and pulled away from my house.

"Nah! Don't worry. I'm glad you told me. It's good for my character bank, you know? Now I know how a paranoid person feels." She laughed shortly. Ruthie was in the Drama Club and was always talking about new characters to sock away in the bank so she could use them for new roles. When she'd first shown an interest in drama, I had tagged along with her and tried out or helped wherever. We quickly realized acting was not one of my talents, and so I had gracefully bowed out. We considered ourselves even since Ruthie had tried basketball for me but dropped out because she had a tendency to help the other team more than ours. We settled for attending each other's events.

"Any new dreams?" Ruthie asked.

After keeping my dreams a secret for so long, it was a relief to be sharing this side of me with her, strange, but nice at the same time.

"Actually, yes." There was only one dream, and I couldn't make heads or tails of it. "But it's even weirder than the last ones."

"Well, out with it."

"Okay. It's about vampires and werewolves."

"Better than cavemen—at least from my point of view." She smiled. "Wait! Werewolves. Wolves in your backyard. Ham shanks! Are we talking about the same thing?"

"Well, maybe. One of the wolves from my backyard looked a lot like the one in my dream..."

"Actually, it's not a big surprise you dreamed about it. I didn't sleep so well myself. It must have scared the meat loaf out of you. Did you wake up your dad?"

"No, thank goodness. The strange thing was that it wasn't as scary as it was sad. Maybe I've seen too many movies, I don't know. I've grown up on this stuff, you know? Anyway, again, I'm watching everything, but not really there. This blonde girl and this big guy, who's pretty hunky, you know, in a Euro-hot way, well, except for the glowing eyes."

Ruthie interrupted me. "Oh please! Glowing eyes? Really. I've seen that movie!"

"I know, right! See why it didn't seem so scary? I kind of knew what was going on."

"What about the girl? Was she a vampire, too?"

"No, they were making out on this beach blanket—"

"That's more my style," Ruthie interjected.

"—And the beach was short, with lots of trees above it. It looked like the edge of a forest—maybe in Canada or something."

"How do you know?"

"I don't, it just looked like those TV shows that film all over the world, you know, showing nature and stuff."

"Never seen them," Ruthie said dismissively.

"Well, anyway, this is when it gets twisted. He suddenly gets a whiff of something that freaks him out, and he twists around hissing with his fangs out just as a wolf streaks out of the trees and leaps down in front of them."

"Been there, seen that! The movie already left the theaters."

"Anyway, it stopped in front of the man and woman and sort of growled and sniffed and stuff. And the vampire guy growled back and hissed at him with his pointy fangs. The girl was looking all scared and hiding behind him."

"Yeah," urged Ruthie.

"Well, the wolf attacked all of a sudden. It was insane! And the vamp and wolf were going at it while the girl screamed."

"Oh my gosh! What happened?" demanded Ruthie.

I could see it clearly in my mind. The man was blonde and pale, his hair long and wavy down to his shoulders, with longer than normal sideburns. His eyes shined like jewels, and they glittered with hatred as he hissed. He was dressed in loose jeans and a long leather jacket. The girl's straight blond hair hung down her back. She wore jeans and a black leather jacket.

At first, they had been playful, laughing and kissing. And then the guy became serious when he said he needed to eat something because she smelled too good. The girl seemed like all those idiots in the movies who think the vampire is so romantic and stuff, but still, she really seemed to love him. She looked like maybe in her twenties. And the guy not much older, but like your typical GQ vampire model.

All of a sudden, the vampire had frozen and looked off toward the forest, his nostrils flaring. He had flipped around at an impossible speed, putting himself between the girl and the wolf who was sticking his head out of the trees sniffing like he was tracking something. When he saw them, he growled and then pounced down upon them. They growled and hissed at each other before attacking. The poor girl had been left with her arms reaching toward the guy, her mouth framing the word "No!"

"Tru! What happened!" Ruthie slapped my knee to pull me back into the present.

"Oh, it was so sad." And it was. The two creatures just about ripped each other apart. And the girl had watched, terrified.

"Um," I continued, "they were all bloody and torn up. It looked like the wolf was winning, too. The wolf had a hold of his shoulder and was just shaking him back and forth really hard. That's when the girl surprised him. I guess she had a pocketknife or something. She snuck up on the wolf and jammed it into his side and jumped back."

"Oh my gosh!"

I suddenly realized we were pulled over to the side of the road, near the area we had seen the wolf before. My eyes scanned the trees.

"Ruthie, we should probably keep going to school."

"I've got to hear this out, girl! I can't drive straight listening to this!"

"Okay. But we better not be late!" I continued the dream. "The wolf dropped the vampire in a pile of dead leaves and turned on the girl, but it didn't seem angry, which is weird because, well, she stabbed it, right?"

"Yeah. But what did the vamp do?"

"The vampire just lay there like he was dead. And the wolf limped slowly up to the girl, who just stood there—I would have run, wouldn't you?" I asked.

"Of course, and screamed, too!"

"Well, the wolf just sniffed her up."

"Ew! That's gross, Tru!"

"No, no. Not like your stupid butt-sniffer dog, Freddy. Geez! No, it kind of smelled up her arm. The wolf was huge, remember. But it didn't seem like it was going to hurt her. Then it licked her cheek and around to the back of her neck, and that's when it bit her."

"What the crap? It *did* bite her? That seems really intentional. Did she die?"

"No. The girl screamed then, and the vampire woke up all covered in leaves and pine needles and pulled himself together enough to knock the wolf away from the girl. In the process, the wolf got his face cut open and then died."

"What? It died? I thought the vamp was dead. Man! Was the girl dead, too?"

"No, she didn't pass out or anything, but she was hurting and crying. The vamp sort of healed, picked her up, and ran off. And that's when I woke up."

"Oh-my-gravy!" Ruthie punctuated each word. "That is so bizarre! But what happened afterward?

This is going to drive me crazy! Will you dream the next episode tonight?"

I gave her a sidelong look. "What do I know? It's something different all the time lately. I don't know what's going on! Can we get to school now?" I asked. Retelling my dream had exhausted me. I felt like I was missing something, that there was more to the dream.

And I still hadn't decided what I was going to do about Zander today.

"Okay, okay." She pulled back on to the road and had to speed to make it on time.

17

FRENEMY

I WAS PREPARED TO face Zander and his lying—albeit very attractive—uh, lips, however, he was a no-show that day. I had gotten nervous for nothing. I didn't have to face him or whatever story he was going to concoct to explain the strangest day of my life. Disappointment, gratitude, and confusion swirled around me as I shut my locker and headed toward Ruthie's. She met me halfway, questions in her eyes.

"So, was he in class?" she asked. He wasn't at lunch and we had begun to suspect he was absent today.

"Not here," I replied.

"Son of a butcher," swore Ruthie.

Zander wasn't the only one MIA today. Isaac and Phoebe missed class, too. When I asked Ruthie about it, she shrugged it off as normal for them. Apparently, they missed school a lot last year, too.

Suddenly, a dark shadow rounded the corner and pounced with a "Raaahwl!" We both jumped, completely caught off guard, screaming instinctively, which in turn startled our attacker, Val, enough that he jumped back into the lockers with a loud clang.

"That was awesome!" guffawed a deep voice from across the way. Jake was doubled over laughing.

"You're a jerk, jerk, JERK!" yelled Ruthie as she began slapping Val's arm.

"Hey! Ow! That's my throwing arm!" wailed Val. He wrapped his arms around her to keep her from beating up on him, laughing at her struggles.

I was still shaken and bent to pick up the books Ruthie and I had dropped. I felt like an idiot. We had definitely overreacted, more victims of our imagination than Val. The tension that had built up all day as I waited to confront Zander had reached its peak, and Val's silly prank had been the final straw. My face was red with mortification. Our screams had attracted the attention of everyone in earshot (which probably included the whole county). Even teachers peered out of their doorways. But after seeing that we were fine and noticing Val in the midst of the trouble, they concluded that it was just a harmless joke.

As I scrambled up, my eyes skimmed the crowds that were returning to whatever they had been doing before all the excitement. One head stood out among all the rest, wavy chestnut hair curling back and blue eyes searching my face with concern.

Speaking of jerks, I thought. There stood the real cause of my stress, and I tacked on public humiliation because all the strange things that had been happening to me seemed to be when I was around him—a sure sign of guilt in my mind at that moment. My hostile glare took him by surprise. His eyebrows shot up and he actually took a step back. *Yeah, be afraid.*

Ruthie finally wriggled free and came to my side. She followed my gaze and added her own fierce scowl.

"They're all jerks," she muttered. "Come on, Tru. We're so out of here." She steered me toward an exit away from Val and Zander.

Kids jeered and yelled out "Scaredy-cat" or "Help! I'm being attacked by the big bad Val!" And it wouldn't be total humiliation without Zena and her harpies pitching in their own disdaining remarks.

"Oh my gosh, Hannah! I think she peed her pants!" Zena quipped as we passed them, which caused everyone to stare you-know-where. I grabbed Ruthie's arm to keep her moving forward when she would have confronted them. Ruthie settled for flipping them a finger behind her back, which gave everyone something else to look at.

We didn't say anything until we got in the car. Then we sighed long and deeply at the same time.

"So Zander *was* at school," stated Ruthie. "Must have been hiding from you."

"But why? His brother made me forget what happened—well, supposedly—so he should have been acting like nothing happened, right?"

"Maybe he just felt guilty. Serves him right, the coward." She started the car. "Man, I'm so breaking up with Val. That was not cool. So not cool."

"Well," I said, "when you stop and think about it, it's not that big of a deal. And it probably looked really funny to everyone else." It seemed somewhat harsh to blame Val for our spastic reactions.

"I know, I know," she said, "I just feel so stupid. I was really scared for a second and, man! I screamed like a little girl!" She laid her head on the steering wheel in defeat. "I thought I was tougher than that, you know?"

"Yeah. I feel stupid, too. But the less we make of it, the faster everyone will forget it, right? If they knew what we've been through, they'd be freaking out, too."

Ruthie turned her head toward me with a smile, but it quickly melted away. She raised her head in surprise, but in seconds covered it up with smooth indifference.

"Uh...don't jump or anything, but your secret boyfriend is standing right outside your window," she whispered, while scratching her nose to cover her moving lips. I froze, my back still to the window.

"What? Oh my gosh, what do I say?"

A knock on the window brought me around. Zander stood looking down at me, his head tilted expectantly, wearing a sexy smile. I must have stared too long because he finally made the motions of rolling down my window. I reminded myself that I was mad at him, that he had allowed his brother to mind-whammy me, and that he was pretending to be a student here. He was up to something, and most importantly, he knew something about my mother's death and wasn't sharing. That final thought brought anger to the front line. I opened the door with a glare.

Ruthie touched my arm and said, "I'll wait right here, okay?"

"Okay, thanks. This shouldn't take long." I stepped out of the car and tried to shrug off my anger. *I should play along,* I thought.

"Uh," Zander paused, "I just wanted to check on you. That was one heck of a scream back there."

I rolled my eyes. "Val being stupid, that's all." I scanned the parking lot behind him looking for his brother.

"Where were you today?" I asked, trying not to sound accusing, but failing.

He took a sudden interest in my sparkly Converse shoes. "My father found a place to rent, and I took the day off to help move stuff in. I just came by at the end to pick up my homework."

"Oh, okay." I pursed my lips, pretty sure he was lying. But man, he was good.

"Speaking of homework," he continued, "can we still get together to study?"

Still? I thought. He was fishing to find out what I remembered. I wanted him to squirm.

"What more do we need to go over? You seemed to understand it really well yesterday at my place." His eyebrows shot up.

"Oh, yeah...well, uh, I just thought the way we left it..." He stopped, giving me an opening to fill in the rest. Nope. I wasn't having any of that. I wanted to hear how *he* filled it in.

"What do you mean?" I asked.

Zander ran a hand through his hair, causing some of it to stick up.

"I was wondering if I could come by again and maybe we could think of a direction for our project?" he asked hopefully.

Perfect, I thought. Answer a question with another question. This was really putting my weak acting skills to the test. But on the other hand, perhaps I could find out more about what *he* knew, too...

"Okay. How about in an hour? I need to finish some other stuff first."

He smiled, and out of nowhere a football came flying toward us. I saw it, but Zander didn't.

I just got out a garbled "Watch—!" before it smacked into his back, knocking him off balance and into me, pushing us up against the car. My head would have smacked against the hood of Ruthie's mini, but one of Zander's hands cushioned it with surprising gentleness. In fact, he was wrapped around me as if he was protecting me. I was held tightly against his chest, and I felt that breathtaking hum along every inch where we touched. I looked up at him and his mouth was inches away from mine, his dark blue eyes boring into me, like soft pools of water. Just then, drowning seemed like a great way to go.

Then the car engine revved. Ruthie's way of saying "time to go." Zander's eyes narrowed and he stepped away after steadying me.

"Are you all right?" he asked.

"Sure," I said softly. "Thanks for the save."

He turned around, saying, "No problem. See you in an hour!" He jogged over to the negligent football and picked it up. Across the parking lot, a group of guys were laughing and pointing at us. Zander pulled back his arm and threw the football. It soared in a perfect spiral directly into the group of boys, plunging into the midsection of the one laughing the loudest. He went down and Zander took off the other way, where he hopped into his brother's waiting truck.

I pulled open the car door and got inside.

"What the ham shank are you doing?" she bellowed. "Hello! Kissy face with the enemy is not good. Yes, he's way hot, but geez! He and his brother erased your memory, girl. Enemy! Not friend!"

I sighed. "Would you be okay with *frenemy?*" I asked with a weary smile. "Looks like I've got another study date this afternoon."

18

Feminine Wiles

AFTER I CALMED RUTHIE down, I explained my great plan to "keep my friends close and my enemies closer" or whatever that quote was. She didn't like it, but since she didn't have a better idea for finding out what he knew, she shrugged and we headed over to my house.

"I know we were all about getting you a guy this year, and I know Zander is way good-looking, but maybe you should focus on one guy at a time, someone normal. Like your Homecoming date!" She gestured madly into the air. Tapping her nails on the steering wheel, she perked up suddenly.

"Hey, we could double date—you and Isaac with Val and me."

I laughed. She was worried about me finding a normal guy. What a flip-turn.

"I thought you were breaking up with Val."

"I might stay with him if we double 'cause that would be fun," she said hopefully.

"Seriously?" I stared at her in wonder. "You would date someone just so we could double?"

"Well, yeah! And I guess I still like Val. I probably won't break up with him." Amusement played along Ruthie's lips. I laughed out loud. "So, what about Isaac? What's up with you two?" she asked softly. "He really does like you."

"I don't know. Yes, he's super cute—"

"And the muscles! Don't forget the muscles!" interjected Ruthie.

I smiled. "And built like a boxer, yes. But, I don't know. Maybe I shouldn't have said yes to Homecoming. I can't imagine kissing him or anything. There's just no zing."

"You mean *hum*," she said knowingly.

"Whatever...moving on..."

"All right, all right. We'll deal with Isaac later. First things first." Ruthie put on a serious face. "Here's the plan. You play up to Zander and get your info, but don't do anything stupid—hey! Is your dad going to be home?"

"I don't know. Probably."

"Well, if he isn't, I could stay, you know, to chaperone." She air-quoted the word "chaperone."

I entertained the thought for a second before shooting it down. There was no way Zander would really tell me what I wanted to know if Ruthie was hanging around. I didn't know if Dad would be okay with Zander coming over to study when he wasn't there, but I didn't want to take the chance that he'd say no. I needed to do this. So one way or the other, Zander was staying, even if I had to lie. My stomach twisted a little. I couldn't remember the last time I lied to my dad. Well, about something like this.

At my house, Ruthie spent at least fifteen minutes teaching me how to play up to Zander, which translated to using my girl power to make his mind mush and get him to slip his secrets. Her words, not mine. Complete crap, had me blushing like crazy, and as far as I could predict, never going to happen. He'd laugh his head off at my "feminine wiles." Ruthie finally left, promising to text me every thirty minutes to make sure I was okay. If I didn't text back, she was coming over, and maybe calling the police even though I insisted she didn't.

I was pacing a hole in our carpet by the time Zander arrived. I had worked up to a whole new level of nervousness as I went over all the reasons why I should not be having this study "date," much less talking to Zander. But it really came down to one thing—I needed to know what he knew about my mother.

Her death was senseless, and I had trouble remembering the night of the accident clearly. My subconscious had blocked out a lot of it—probably a survival tactic. It was too awful to remember. No one should have to watch a parent die.

So, my need to "know" was becoming an obsession, spurring me to go way beyond my comfort level. How was I going to pretend I didn't remember and still ask questions? Should I tell him I remembered? Would he confide in me? Who was he really? And werewolves? What the heck?

When the doorbell rang, I made one last look in the entry hall mirror. My hair hung in its normal sunny waves down to my waist. Nothing fancy, but I would do. My eyes seemed golden brown today. Despite my summer tan, I was still a little pale by California standards. How does one dress for this situation? Who knew? And when you don't know, T-shirt and jeans is always the answer, or that's what I thought. I had second thoughts about the T-shirt I chose, but went with it in the end. The words "BITE ME" across my chest summed up my attitude at this point, and it filled me with courage because it was a gift from Ruthie. Yeah, it was old and ratty now, but thinking of Ruthie and her "advice" gave me the audacity I needed.

Zander stood on my doorstep, his backpack slung over one shoulder. His face brightened with a smile.

"Hey...uh..." He darted glances down at my shirt. "Nice shirt."

My face flamed. I really was a moron. "Bite Me" could be interpreted a couple different ways. Just proved how messed up my head was right now. He probably thought I was making a move on him or something.

"Oh. Thanks. It's kind of stupid, I know." I pulled on the hem of the shirt, trying to make it seem less tight, but failing. I was close to crossing my arms over my chest, but realized that it would just make my discomfort more obvious.

"No, really," he said. "I like the attitude. It reminds me of my best friend. He's pretty unconventional."

Relieved that he got the intended meaning, I stopped slouching.

"Actually, Ruthie gave it to me. Attitude is kind of her thing. Maybe we should introduce them sometime."

"Sounds good except that he didn't move here with me."

"Oh, right!" I laughed with chagrin. "Where did you say you lived before?"

"Actually, I didn't say. But it's a small town up in Washington State. You wouldn't know it."

"Probably right," I said. "I bet you miss your friend." Going back to school without Ruthie would have killed me.

A breeze swept through the overhead trees and across the front porch. My hair flew up unexpectedly.

"Agh!" I shrieked, laughing as I tried to tame the long strands that swept up and all over both Zander and me. He laughed, too, as he disentangled us. His hands smoothed my hair down, one hand returning to my face. I looked into his eyes at the same moment.

Breathing him in, I leaned closer. He gently traced one of my eyebrows, his other hand coming up to trace the other. His thumbs brushed over my lips.

He paused as our signature hum enveloped us like an ocean wave, unbalancing, and stealing our air. For the first time, we didn't pull away from it, and the feeling settled into a mellow vibration.

We both gasped for air at the same time, staring at each other in astonishment. Then he lowered his lips, grazing the corner of my mouth and brushing across me experimentally. My eyes fluttered closed. His touch ignited something inside me, and then his lips took over mine as he pushed me through the doorway, pressing me up against the wall. My hands traveled around his neck, one hand in his hair.

Suddenly, the sound of Katy Perry blared out of my pocket, and my eyes popped open. Zander was staring down at me from the front porch, his hand still on my cheek, and not even a hint of a breeze in the air.

Wait a second! Didn't we move into the house? Didn't we just share an amazing kiss? What just happened?

Katy Perry's voice sounded again, singing about a magnetizing touch, bodies glowing, and futuristic lovers.

Zander dropped his hand. "You better get that." His face was pink, his eyebrows pushed together.

Ruthie had set a new ringtone for me today with a secretive laugh and said it was a surprise. I was so busy thinking about my problems that I shrugged it off. Now I knew why she thought it so hilarious. Her choice of ringtone and her timing couldn't be more wrong and perfect at the same time.

I stepped into the house, opening the door wide to allow Zander's entrance. I mumbled, "Sorry!" and walked unsteadily into the kitchen to answer.

"Nice one, Ruthie," I said a little breathlessly.

"Ha! I thought you'd like it. Why do you sound so weird?" She was suspicious. "Are you all right? Is *he* there yet?"

"I'm fine." I laughed uneasily. "Yes. Just studying away right now." I was very conscious of Zander a few feet away. Inside, I was reeling. What just happened? I wondered if I should have Ruthie come over after all. I sneaked a quick glance back at him. He was rubbing a hand down his face, looking a little dazed. *Okay,* I thought. Maybe he was thrown a little, too. But I had to keep my eye on the ball this time. My goal was to get information, not fall for the guy. The grief that always came whenever I thought of my mother snapped me out of my bewilderment.

Zander was in the middle of making an unplanned exit.

"Wait!" I called out to him.

He paused and scowled at me, which caused me to step back. What had I done? I was suddenly angry. Best daydream ever and he was going to take off and make me feel like an idiot. At least we hadn't really kissed. We hadn't, right?

"Tru! Tru! Hello!" Ruthie was practically yelling in the phone. I had tuned her out. "You are so not okay. I'm coming over right now."

"Ruthie, no! Everything is fine." I made a quick beeline for the front steps, placing myself between Zander and his getaway. "Chill out, girl!" I put up my hand and wrapped up my phone call. I never knew I could multitask so well.

"What the heck are you doing?" I demanded, my chest heaving. I didn't want him to leave, but how were we going to study now? How was I going to get him to talk?

"What do you mean me?" Zander stepped back. "What was all *that*?" He waved toward the entry hall, where we had "not kissed." I was never going to be able to look at it again without thinking of him. Did he have the same daydream as me? Was that possible? A bright red blush stole up my cheeks, and deepened the more I thought about the possibility. This was so embarrassing.

"I have no idea what you are talking about." I was being unfair, but he just made me so mad!

His eyebrows shot up, like he couldn't believe his ears.

"You don't even know what you're doing, do you?" he said.

"Huh? Seriously, you aren't making any sense." Now he was talking crazy, and I couldn't even connect it to the other crazy talk he and his brother did yesterday. This was so not going like I planned.

He glanced down at the floor.

"Look. I'm sorry about...whatever." He waved his hand around. He swung his backpack over his shoulder and brushed past. "I've got to go. There's something important I need to take care of. I'll see you tomorrow, okay?"

And he was gone.

19

JEALOUSY

I DON'T KNOW HOW long Zander had been gone when I heard the doorbell. I was just wandering around the kitchen, speculating about what he could have been talking about, and I was angry, really angry.

Oh no, I thought. Ruthie probably drove over because I didn't text her. I had turned my cell phone to vibrate until I changed the ringtone.

I rushed to the door as the bell pealed again. But the person standing on my doorstep was not my best friend. Instead, it was a fuming Isaac Efoti. His face purple, shoulders curved up, fists on his hips, and thunder on his face. I backed up.

"Uh. Hi, Isaac. What's up?" I said, pulling the door closed a little.

I could have sworn I heard a low growl come from his mouth. Really? There had been way too much growling around this house lately, I thought.

"What was *he* doing here?" Isaac snarled.

"Whoa, there! What's wrong with you? Are you okay?" It occurred to me that I knew next to nothing about him, mostly what Ruthie had told me since school started.

He stepped forward, forcing the door open and me backward, but he followed me and breathed in deeply.

"You smell like him." His voice was like gravel.

I tried to move away, stepping back into the kitchen. But he stuck to me like a shadow, scowling and kicking the door shut behind him. When did my own home stop feeling like the safest place on earth?

"Isaac," I said cajolingly, putting my hand up as if to ward him off. "I don't know what's going on, but I think you should leave. You're scaring me, big-time."

My words must have sunk in, because he paused, visibly making an attempt to calm himself by closing his eyes and letting go of my arm. I didn't realize until then that he'd grabbed me.

"Ouch!" I said belatedly. I was going to have a bruise.

He looked down at my arm and winced.

"Tru, I'm sorry! I swear I don't know what happened!" With a disgusted mutter, he put some distance between us by moving further into the kitchen. He hunched over the sink and stared into the backyard.

"You must think I'm an animal," he said.

"Right now I think you're a jerk!" My fright had vanished and suddenly I was mad. Who did he think he was? "Are you on drugs or something?" Seriously, nothing else made sense.

Something between a cough and a laugh forced itself out of Isaac's mouth. "No. Just not myself for a second." He turned to face me. "Uh, I guess I have a temper problem."

"No kidding." I rubbed my sore arm. He watched me with those sad puppy dog eyes. Now I was feeling sorry for him. Man, he was good.

"So, what let the beast out?" I snapped. I was really regretting our Homecoming plans.

This seemed to set him off again, but it sounded like he was truly amused. I decided he was bipolar and resolved to break off our date as soon as he stopped the Jekyll and Hyde act.

"Good one, Parker," he snorted. "Man, you have no idea. I like your shirt, by the way."

"Screw you!" I was done with this. "What's your problem, really? Why are you here? And most importantly, how soon can you leave?"

"Hey! I'm sorry! But I was mad—and I'm still kind of mad." *This* anger I could handle. He seemed more like the Isaac I was used to. He rubbed the back of his neck, sighing, and began again. "I missed y—*school* today and, and thought I would drop by to see you." He turned back to look out the window. "I saw Zander leaving your house," he continued in a strained voice, "and well, I just kind of blew a fuse. But I probably jumped to the wrong conclusions, like I seem to be doing all the time these days. Phoebe is always getting on my case about that."

He was rambling. I could hear the shame in his voice. Now I was ashamed, and could feel the heat creep up my neck. Although I had not planned it, nor did I understand it, *something* had occurred between Zander and me. And it had been explosive and unforgettable. That attraction I'd felt toward "Hottie Efoti" on the first day of school was just gone, and I realized it had never been more than admiration. That realization was surprising in itself. But, while I didn't know what was going on between Zander and me, I didn't discount the idea that I wanted something to be going on. However, I didn't know if Zander would be around tomorrow, much less be here for Homecoming. He certainly hadn't left me with any ideas that he wanted anything to be going on between us. He had just left me confused, on many levels. Sadness swept through me.

In the meantime, I had a problem if Isaac thought he and I were together—together, as in a couple.

"Isaac, I think there's been a misunderstanding—"

"That's what I thought! I'm so glad!" He beamed and walked up close to me, grabbing for my hand, and for the first time since he arrived, he really looked at me. *Man, he is super tall,* I thought.

"Hey, are you all right?" he asked. I must have looked traumatized.

Isaac's big hands cradled my face. I could feel their strength and thought it would only take a second for him to snap my neck. A burst of fear had me backing away.

"Whoa, Tru, I won't hurt you, I promise," he pleaded. "Are you okay? Did Zander do something to hurt you?" He was battling the anger again.

"No!" I put up a hand. "No, it's not that. I-I was just—" What could I say? For once, I brought up my mom. "I was just thinking about my mom, you see, and—"

"Oh. That's okay, then." He stopped himself. "I mean it's not okay that you're sad and all, just that I'm glad you aren't hurt; not that you aren't hurting, just that—"

I laughed as he kept backpedaling and making it sound worse.

"Isaac. It's fine. I'm not going to freak out if you mention her." And I realized I wasn't going to for the first time in a long time. I smiled at that thought. Yes!

Isaac sighed loudly. "Thank goodness!" He returned my smile. And the next thing I knew he was pulling me closer.

"Wait! Not so fast, mister." I pushed back. He looked wretchedly hopeful and what I wanted to say felt mean. He stared down at me with just the right amount of insecurity in his eyes to make me forget what I was going to say. I certainly didn't want to hurt him.

I didn't want to make him mad, either, because that went over so well already. So I took the coward's path and I tried to distract him. "Why did you guys miss school today, anyway?" He leaned back against the counter again, folding his arms. His face closed in. I got the feeling he didn't want to talk about it.

"Family thing. My uncle is visiting."

"Nice. Wish I got to skip school for something like that," I said, trying to lighten things up. I didn't think my dad would ever let me skip school to visit with Uncle Ira.

"Actually, Phoebe and I didn't want to miss school. But, well, our folks are real sticklers about *family duty.*" He made family duty sound like a chore, which, now that I thought about it, was true for most kids I knew.

"Okay," I said, hoping he'd forgotten the reason he was in my house in the first place. "My dad should be getting home soon, and you probably shouldn't be here."

"What about Zander?" He wasn't budging until he got an explanation. I sighed, not wanting to have this conversation with him right now. His angry fit had freaked me out. I smiled sheepishly at that thought. Oh, the irony. A week ago I was worried about everyone else thinking I was loony. Had it really only been that long?

Isaac was back to scowling. "Tru."

"Oh, uh—" The doorbell rang again. That must be Ruthie. For the first time today I was grateful for her interruption.

"Hang on a second," I said to Isaac, but he ignored me and shadowed my steps. Territorial, seriously!

I yanked open the door. Wow. It was now officially a party. Ruthie and Phoebe stood on the porch. They looked anxiously behind me. Phoebe glared at Isaac, and Ruthie stretched to see over us, probably looking for Zander.

I sighed heavily. "Come on in."

The four of us sat around my living room, sipping the sodas that Ruthie had grabbed for us. The only good thing was Isaac couldn't bother me about Zander in front of Ruthie and his sister. Phoebe and Ruthie caught up on school gossip, with me throwing in an occasional "yeah" and "no kidding." Isaac didn't contribute anything, which just made Ruthie talk faster—she did that when she was nervous. Phoebe was still glaring at Isaac while he sulked in my dad's leather La-Z-Boy. He stared out the window, but wasn't as impervious to her as he attempted to demonstrate, because his grip on the arms of the chair made me concerned for my dad's favorite seat in the house.

Ruthie rambled on about coming over to get help with algebra, and how on the way she had run into

Phoebe walking up the street, so she'd brought her along. I rolled my eyes and looked pointedly at her empty hands. She was conspicuously missing said homework. But the other two didn't seem to notice. I was wondering why Phoebe had been walking up my street in the first place. Had she been with Isaac when he saw Zander? Had they both seen Zander? Why did I even care?

"So," continued Ruthie with a singsong voice, "I guess Phoebe knew Isaac was coming over and thought she would join you guys, right?" She looked at Phoebe, but she didn't seem to hear.

"Hel-l-o!" Ruthie waved her hand toward Phoebe to get her attention.

Phoebe finally looked at us, but she still looked mad. "What?" she snapped.

"I-I was just telling Tru why you were with me. Geez, girl!"

Phoebe looked startled for a second, but then calmed. "Oh, yeah. Sorry. What I told you. Yeah. Heard there was an after-school party here or something." She flipped her glossy hair over her shoulder and leaned back into the sofa. "And if there wasn't, I thought I could start one." She grinned conspiratorially. Ruthie and I looked at her blankly.

"O-kay," she continued. "Looks like I need to get one going." She pulled out her phone and started flipping through numbers.

"Whoa, there!" I jumped up and grabbed her phone. "I'm not having a party here! My dad would kill me!"

"Then we'll keep it small," Phoebe coaxed. "Just the four of us."

"Oooh. Make that five. I'll call Val," gushed Ruthie, pulling out her phone.

I snatched her phone, too, and just for good measure, knocked her upside the head.

"Ow!"

"No! Seriously, people, no party!" Ruthie was easily distracted, but still! Had she forgotten why she had come over in the first place? I could see that was the case by her look of chagrin. I shook my head, exasperated.

"I've got homework. It's the middle of the week. My dad will be home any minute. Oh, and another: I'm not in the partying mood!" I stomped off to the kitchen and sat at the table, staring at my homework and wondering how much crazier my day could get. I wished they would all leave.

Ruthie pulled up a chair and leaned over to whisper, "Sorry, girl. My ADD again." She leaned in and bumped my shoulder with her own.

I appreciated the gesture. Setting the phones on the table, I leaned my elbow on my textbook and rested my head in my upraised hand. I whispered back to Ruthie so Phoebe and Isaac wouldn't hear. "Thanks for coming. Good timing, actually." I rolled my eyes back toward the living room.

"That must have been close! What happened with Z?" she murmured, barely moving her lips. I cracked a smile at her because she was so obvious. It reminded me of all the old times when we tried to speak secretly in front of our parents. It usually didn't work. Thank goodness the two in the living room were too far away to hear our not-so-covert conversation. They were sitting quietly, looking away from us. They really were strange sometimes.

Angling away from the twins again, I replied, "Isaac saw Zander leave and was seriously ticked when he came over. What is up with that?!"

"Uh oh! Not good." Her sneaky whispering just seemed to bring more attention to her. "So what happened with Z? Did you get any new info?"

"I didn't get a chance."

"What?" Ruthie raised her voice. "Oh, sorry," she murmured.

I glanced back at the twins. Their stiff poses made me uncomfortable. If I didn't know they couldn't possibly hear me, I would think they were listening. Maybe they were doing that twin thing again.

"What happened then? You seriously didn't talk about the *wolves?*" She said the word so lightly, I barely heard her. Isaac and Phoebe stood up suddenly, Phoebe holding Isaac back from rushing over to us. He was back to ferocious boy.

"I'll have to tell you later," I said out of the side of my mouth.

"Sorry, Tru." Phoebe pulled her brother toward the door. "Our dad just texted us. We have to get home."

I held out her cell phone. "But I have your phone right here."

"Oh, yeah. Almost forgot that. Uh, Isaac got the text. Can you toss me my phone?" I think Isaac was growling. For some reason, he reminded me of one of my neighbor's dogs that they had to hold on to every time someone walked by their house.

"Seriously?"

"Yeah, you have a good arm. Send it!"

I tossed it to her and she snagged it out of the air like a Frisbee.

"Piece of cake. We will have to get together another time. See you." Isaac scowled all the way to the door, but just as he passed through, he shot a suspicious look back at me. Despite his strange behavior, guilt weighed heavily in my stomach.

20

Fake Fuzzies

As soon as the front door slammed, Ruthie whirled around on me.

"Man! I thought they'd never leave!"

"Yeah, I thought they were weirder than normal."

Ruthie shrugged. "They've always been that way. So, now you can tell me what really happened. And I know something happened. My scoop antenna is going crazy!" She rubbed her hands together gleefully.

I shoved away from the table, not in the mood to divulge anything. I really needed to think about this. And I was still kind of frustrated with her for her immature attitude toward my situation.

"You really need to work on your improv—I mean really! You came over for math help, without your math book?" I grabbed another soda out of the fridge. "And then there was that stupid ringtone! Seriously, that was totally awkward for me!"

I stared out the kitchen window.

A chair scraped across the floor. An arm curved around my shoulders. Strawberry-scented hair tickled my neck as Ruthie brought her other arm around me for a side-hug.

"Hey, girl, I guess I flunk at being your BFF today. I'm such an airhead sometimes."

I struggled to maintain my disgust with her, but too many years with her zaniness, her constant friendship during the worst time of my life, and the fact that I knew she really did care about me, washed away my irritation and I leaned my cheek down to her head.

"I know. Sorry I'm being the Anti-BFF right now. I'm just so confused."

Back up in my bedroom, I filled her in on everything. Even the daydream kiss. Predictably, Ruthie congratulated my smooth moves like a proud mama and announced we were going to celebrate my non-virgin lips with ice cream and streamers. I pointed out first that technically I hadn't really kissed Zander, just imagined it, and second, that Isaac kissed me first, and third, that ice cream was for depression. But she rebutted by stating that the jury was still out regarding the "daydream kiss," public kisses didn't count (although, Isaac's might change her mind), and she insisted that ice cream was a food suitable for depression and happiness.

"But I'm not happy about it," I admitted. "And I wasn't really doing a good job at the seduction thing. I was actually pretty lame."

"Yeah, that's why you were dream-locking lips like Han Solo and Princess Leia," she smirked.

I laughed at the thought of her watching *Star Wars.*

"Hey!" she defended. "The show has its moments. Besides, I've got two geeky brothers, remember? It's a sure way to keep them from wrecking the house and stop them from totally annoying me."

"It wasn't like that." But in my head, I was thinking that maybe it was like that. "I mean," I continued, "I don't know what happened. It was almost like we had the same dream. He seemed messed up, too. In fact, he seemed angry, like I did something, which is—" I flicked my arms angrily, "well, it's just stupid, crazy, inconceivable!"

"All right, now. Just calm down. You're starting to use big words and you know how I hate that." Ruthie leaned back against my bed pillows while I paced. "Let's look at what we've got here. There's Zander and all his hotness. He's mysterious. He's some kind of secret soldier dude. He's here to find out about the accident that—" She coughed. "Well, *The Accident.*" She air-quoted the words and used a soft voice, probably afraid to send me into tears. But again, I was amazed that the reference to my mother didn't spur the usual bout of sadness.

Ruthie continued. "Then there's Zander's *Terminator* slash *Commando* brother wearing—you said military clothes, right?"

I nodded.

"You should have guessed he was the bad guy just because of that, but anyway, you say he mind-whammied you, right? Tried to erase your memories. So. Yeah. One seriously evil guy who happens to be related to your dream-kissing study buddy."

I rolled my eyes. Yet, the reminder caused heat to rush up my neck.

"And..." I prompted.

"Well, you add that to the mind-boggling idea that there were a couple of werewolves running around your backyard and the dreams about vampires and werewolves and cave people."

I stopped pacing to stare at her.

"And..." I said again.

"If Zander's brother can do things to people's brains, it stands to reason that maybe Zander can, too, right?"

What? Why hadn't I thought of that? That could explain so much.

"Oh my gosh, Ruthie! You mean Zander could have made me imagine kissing him like that?" My heart turned over in denial. "Maybe he makes me feel that hum thingie, too!" I sank to the floor as the ramifications flooded my mind and my heart. What if I didn't really have a crush on him? It would make so much sense because I did have a bit of a crush on Isaac before Zander showed up. Ruthie was totally on the same page as me.

"No wonder poor Isaac is feeling jealous, girl! He's starting to notice you and Zander and all your warm fuzzies for each other! But what if they are fake fuzzies?"

"Yeah... Now I don't feel as stupid for being confused." But I was starting to feel stupid for an entirely new reason. I felt manipulated and hurt and horrified. It ticked me off.

"So, what are you going to do, Tru? You still need to find out about the accident, right?"

I worried my bottom lip. What were my options? Tell Zander to take a flying leap and give Isaac and me a chance? My stomach twisted at the idea, but I told myself it was some mind control thing and that if Zander hadn't entered my life, I would probably be enjoying a healthy and normal high school romance with one of the best-looking guys in school and moving on from my horrible last year.

However, if Zander hadn't entered my life, I would never know that there was so much more to my mother's accident, that the supernatural creatures in the movies were actually real, or at least some of them.

And I wouldn't have this chance to find out what really happened to her.

"Agh! I don't know, Ruthie!" I felt like tearing my hair out. "As much as I'd like to at the moment..." I paused. Bubbling up from the bottom of a whole lot of rational reasons to dislike Zander was the truth that despite his behavior, I didn't dislike him. And I didn't dislike him a lot. But I continued to squelch the thought.

I stared into Ruthie's big brown eyes, knowing that panic and confusion were pouring out of mine. "Ruthie, I can't stop hanging out with Zander because he's the only connection I have to the accident. And if the whatever-you-want-to-call-it thing between us is fake and I should be more into Isaac, then I don't want to be a total pawn, you know?"

Ruthie blew a puff of air out of her lips as they twisted ruefully. "So true. You can't let them have all the control. But," a sparkle popped back into Ruthie's hazel eyes, "what if you try to just be study buddies with Zander? He wants to keep you around, right? To figure out what's going on in your backyard, right? So, he'll probably take whatever you give him. That's what I'm thinking. And then it frees you up to see how things go with Isaac!"

"Okay. But what if I'm still having these feelings for Zander and it totally messes up things with Isaac?"

"Since you know it's not real between you and Zander, maybe it won't have such an effect on you anymore." She looked hopeful.

I felt doubtful, but I didn't see another choice. I'd have to give it a try.

That night, Ruthie gave me a new mantra to repeat every morning in front of the mirror.

"Zander is a fake. The hum is humdrum. Zander probably has a girlfriend where he comes from. Isaac really likes me and I like him."

She wanted me to say "love him" but I just couldn't get the words out of my mouth. So I was going to *like* him like crazy!

21

SHADOWS

I EXPECTED ZANDER TO at least put up a fight, something. But no, he thought "friendship" was the perfect way to describe what we had, and meeting in the school library to finish our English project was just fine. I had agonized for hours wondering how to confront him about it. I mean, how do you say "let's just be friends" to the guy you secretly crave every hour of the day? And I wasn't even sure he wanted anything more anyway. But he had picked up my line of thinking quickly and had taken it to the bank. I had to lock myself in the bathroom stall until I stopped crying. It was like we were breaking up, which was stupid. I was so stupid. And yet, there it was. If he wanted to be friends, why was he making me want so much more?

THE STRESS OF IGNORING my feelings was beginning to really get to me. I was becoming paranoid, feeling like someone was always watching me. The back of my neck would tingle at the oddest times, and when I looked around, I couldn't find anyone actually staring. I kept hoping it was Zander, hoping that he wanted to be more than friends. But then I'd chide myself and recite my new mantra. Fake, fake, fake!

Once in a while, I did catch someone looking back—Isaac. But I didn't think he was causing my paranoia. However, he was causing my annoyance. He was constantly parking in my personal space. More than once, he walked me to drama with his arm around my shoulders. I felt branded. Maybe that's why I felt like I was being watched—everyone at school was staring. At us, the new, shiny couple. They were wondering what he saw in me, no doubt.

I knew I had promised Ruthie that I was going to give Isaac a chance, but it just didn't feel right. After the first lunch when Isaac pulled me into his lap, Zander started eating lunch at a new table. For a few minutes, he sat alone, but then the vultures moved in and claimed him like road kill. Zena artfully bullied the flock until she was curling her own arm around his. Every time she touched him it seemed like she was writing "MINE" in Sharpie pen. Yeah, of all the girls in school, and there were a lot of them, it had to be her. My lunch started to back up when I saw their heads bent toward each other, and I began to eat less and less at lunch time.

I wasn't the only one to notice Zander's new fans. Phoebe looked a little heartbroken herself. I could understand her pain. However, one person seemed ready to celebrate his departure from our table—Isaac. He was as happy as Ruthie at the mall on Black Friday. But Phoebe wasn't neglected by any means. She had plenty of admirers zeroing in on her.

So, by the weekend, I was officially "Hottie Efoti's girlfriend" (Ruthie's label had spread), and I was the awe and envy of the entire female population at SVHS, except Zena, who was deliriously happy draped all over Zander. Ruthie was thrilled beyond words Friday when she dropped me off at home. She said she was dropping major hints to Val about Homecoming and expected him to ask her any day.

I just couldn't shake my obsession with Zander, though. I woke up every night during dreams involving Zander, some quite embarrassing, to be honest. I felt guilty about them every time I talked to Isaac, who called every day over the weekend, even showed up with Phoebe and pizza Sunday afternoon to hang out. Later, Ruthie and Val came over and we watched movies until late.

Thank goodness Dad was home. He walked through the living room a million times with pointed looks at Isaac, who took the hint and kept his hands to himself. If I had not been so thankful, I would have laughed at Isaac's frustration. Phoebe could not contain her humor, though. Isaac shot quite a few fierce looks her way, to which Ruthie kept inquiring, "What's going on?" or "Hey, let me in on the joke!"

Dad, the "watchdog," was taking his job seriously. He even stood next to me as I said good night. Isaac had to settle for a friendly wave. Ruthie and Val took off at the same time, although she gave the "call me later" hand signal as she stepped into her Mini. Isaac and Phoebe took off in their dad's truck. I was exhausted but didn't look forward to closing my eyes. I wondered how long it would take to get Zander out of my head.

By Monday morning, dark circles underlined my eyes. Guilt, strange dreams, and all the weird events over the past few weeks were wearing me down. I just wanted to stay home and feel sorry for myself. Could I even do that?

22

Game Changer

Ruthie looked extra fine this morning when she picked me up. I smiled at her as she cheerfully explained her plan to nudge Val into inviting her to Homecoming.

"Did you ask your dad to pick you up from school today?" Ruthie asked. "Because I don't want to leave you stranded."

"Oh, yeah, he's picking me up." I laughed. "I wouldn't dare mess with *Operation Homecoming!*" She giggled at the name I had given her scheme.

After everyone had left the night before, Ruthie called me to discuss how she would manipulate things the next day with Val, starting with looking as hot as possible, pulling him aside for a private lunch, which would just happen to be under a homecoming sign, which would make it simple to bring up the topic of who was going with whom, which would inevitably cause her to speculate on who she might go with, dropping a few names and batting her long black eyelashes. If he didn't ask her after that or at least give her a hint about his intentions, then she was going to go find another guy and try the jealousy route. Either way, she planned to stay after school and watch his football practice like a good girlfriend. There were plenty other football players to use for the jealousy angle, if needed.

I had no interest in ogling football players after school. Ruthie told me to catch a ride with Isaac, but I didn't want to join him. I had a plan of my own: to break things off with Isaac. It just didn't feel right and I was finally going to follow my instincts, which said Isaac was not for me. Besides, he was not the one who was filling my thoughts night and day. And I was pretty sure Zander was no longer compelling me to like him, if he ever was. No, I was just messed up.

Because I knew how Ruthie would react, I had not told her yet. I just wasn't up for her drama today, and fortunately Ruthie was so occupied with *Operation Homecoming*, she hadn't picked up on my slightly depressed state of mind or the dark circles under my eyes.

"Good gravy!" Ruthie exclaimed, rubbing her hands together. "This is going to be an awesome day!"

"Just keep your hands on the wheel, Sophia," I admonished her, as the car edged out of our lane. She laughed. It had been a long time since I had called her that. I told her once that she was like Sophia Loren, curvy and beautiful. Plus, they shared the same coloring.

"No problema, chica!" The car swerved back into the lane.

As we walked out of the school parking lot, a chill went up my neck as I again felt someone watching me. I peered around but didn't see anyone staring back. I couldn't shake that feeling, though, as I sped up to class.

By the time lunch rolled around, I stalled at my locker, wondering how to avoid Isaac. I needed to talk to him in private, but I wasn't sure if I should speak to him about us at school or wait until afterward. I had seen him freaked out before, and I didn't want a repeat performance in public. Maybe I could catch him after school before my dad showed up. I definitely didn't want to break up with him alone; I needed potential witnesses around me. The fact that I felt I needed that kind of protection gave me the additional reassurance that I was doing the right thing. Perhaps I could go study in the library. Ruthie wasn't going to miss me today, not with her lunch plans. I made up my mind and took off down the hall.

"Tru, wait up!"

I knew that voice even before I turned around. It was like my silk pajamas, smooth and soft. A sigh went through me and I turned around.

"Zander." I smiled as he pulled up beside me.

"Where are you headed? Skipping lunch today?" he asked, reciprocating my smile.

"Yeah. I thought I would study in the library today."

"Mind if I join you? Maybe we could finish up our English project." He raised an eyebrow.

"Um," I hesitated, allowing a debate to rage in my mind at warp speed as I continued walking and staring at the floor. Despite the watered-down suspicion that he might be creating this need in me, I couldn't deny him any longer. Maybe if it *looked* and *felt* like a crush, it *was* a crush, not some mind-whammy thing like we thought. I'd never believed in the kind of obsessive love you saw in the movies or read about in those steamy romance novels (not that I read them; Ruthie read them to me, of course). But what if it could happen? Yeah, Zander was a risky, with his weird brother and mysterious origins, but dang! Why couldn't I just enjoy whatever this was?

Then I remembered my mother.

"Or, maybe you should eat something. You look pretty hungry."

I raised one eyebrow. What was he talking about?

His smile widened. "You're chewing your lips off." I cupped a hand over my mouth as he shrugged off his backpack, pulling out a granola bar.

"Here. Eat up."

Great. Circles under my eyes and now red, swollen lips. I bit them sometimes when I was stressed.

"Thanks, but I have some stuff in my backpack. I'm just stressed about...uh...my history paper..."

Zander shrugged. "Okay. Want some help? I'm pretty good in history."

Why couldn't I find out what happened to my mom while letting this thing between Zander and me develop however it might? Zander gave me another questioning look. Man, his eyelashes were long.

"Sure," I agreed finally. "Sounds like a plan!"

Both of us stayed clear of any conversation related to Isaac or what might be going on at the lunch tables. I talked him out of helping with history because my paper was already printed up and ready to hand in, and steered him toward our English project. In fifteen minutes we had the conclusion written. Now we just needed a rewrite and a bibliography. The awkwardness of last week was mostly gone, and conversation moved to more personal topics.

"So, what are you going to do after high school, Tru?" Zander peered at me with genuine interest, the white flecks in his midnight blue eyes making them sparkle. They warmed me from the inside out.

"College, of course. Isn't everyone?" I wondered what he was doing.

"That sounds great, actually. I haven't exactly talked to my father about it, though."

"Seriously?" My jaw almost dropped to the table. "I thought all parents wanted their kids to go to college. Or, maybe your dad is looking at military for you?" If he was some super agent, then that made total sense.

"I guess you could say that. It's kind of a family tradition." He drummed his fingers on the table.

"Well, that doesn't sound like a good reason to not go to college, if you want that. What do you want to study?"

"I always wanted to go into some kind of medical career, but I don't think my father will go for it."

"Can't you get trained as a doctor in the military?"

"Yeah, I guess so."

"But your dad doesn't like that idea?"

"No..."

"Oh, your dad doesn't even know you're interested in a medical career?"

He smiled grimly. Bingo.

He didn't seem very enthusiastic about the military. I wondered what kind of military his dad was in. Then I remembered his brother. We hadn't ever talked about what I remembered from that day in my backyard. For some reason, I really wanted to now. For the first time I felt connected with the real him. I felt that he might give me some honest answers.

"Zander, the last time we studied at my house..." I began. I peeked into his face. His face had tightened and his face flushed. Once again I wondered if he could have had the same daydream or whatever it was as I had. I quickly backpedaled.

I ran a hand through my hair as if to ward off the memory, but it didn't prevent my face from flaming out. "I mean the time your brother came over..." I let that sink in for a second. Yeah, that got a different reaction from him.

Zander sat up straight. "Tru! You do remember what happened, don't you?"

Just then the warning bell rang. We both groaned, wanting to keep talking.

I pulled up one side of my mouth, "Yeah. I do. I remember the wolves, the guns, and your stupid brother."

"Why didn't you say something before now?"

I just shrugged. "I was waiting for you to say something first."

Zander grabbed his backpack and looked around the room.

"We need to talk, now." He grabbed my arm and I barely snagged up my backpack before he was pulling me through the librarian's office and through a door leading out of the school.

"Now? Are you crazy?" I demanded. "We are going to get caught!" I'd never skipped school before, much to Ruthie's chagrin. She would have loved a partner in crime.

He clenched his jaw and propelled us both down the sidewalk behind the school.

"This is important, Tru," he said, looking around a corner before pulling me across the gap between buildings. We were still a decent distance from the parking lot, where he seemed to be dragging me.

Just then, a door opened behind us, and a voice bellowed, "Hey!" It was Coach Dean, the football coach and biology teacher. His voice was loud and booming. "What do you two think you are doing?"

Zander stopped with a large sigh and a muttered "Great!" He turned toward me. Our eyes connected and his went wide suddenly. He leaned in and whispered, "Do you think you can *convince* him to just forget about us?" His eyebrows lifted when he said "convince."

"Huh?" I whispered back, totally confused. "Seriously, Zander, I'm a terrible liar, really! We are so busted!"

Zander blew air out through clenched teeth. "Worth a try," he muttered.

The coach's voice rose louder. "Yeah, I'm talking to you two."

We turned around.

"Parker?" Coach Dean sounded surprised to see me.

"Uh, yes, sir." My record was so squeaky clean, I'm sure the coach was shocked to see me trying to ditch class with a boy.

He walked up closer to us. "And your name, young man?" He looked Zander over, appraisingly. I knew what he saw—football potential. Coaches were always looking for recruits, and they always catered to team players. They got away with murder at school. Maybe he would go lightly on us, I hoped.

"Zander Hughes, sir."

I realized that this was the first time I had heard Zander's last name. I felt stupid. I really had a lot to learn about the guy who occupied my thoughts so much.

"You new at this school, Hughes?" asked the coach.

Here we go, I thought.

"Yes, sir." Zander stood at attention, looking the coach in the eye.

"Ever played football?"

"Yes, sir, but not on a team."

"Hmm... And where were you two planning to go?"

"I know it looks inappropriate, sir, but we were just heading to my car to work on our English project because we are behind on it and we couldn't meet after school. I'm sorry. We shouldn't have tried to ditch, even to do homework."

I just nodded my head, agreeing with everything he said. *Nice excuse,* I thought. He sounded so sorry. I knew Coach was going to buy it, especially if he hoped to recruit Zander for his team.

Coach looked from Zander to me, and back again. He seemed to come to a decision.

"Well, now. Studying is a worthy pursuit, but not good enough to skip class. As long as you don't do it again..." We nodded our heads. "Okay, I've held you up long enough. You'll be tardy for class now. Why don't you two follow me and I'll write up some excuses for you before you head back."

"Thank you, sir," both Zander and I chorused. I was smiling smugly, but Zander appeared annoyed. We definitely wouldn't be having our discussion now. But at least we weren't going to be punished for trying to skip class. I felt like I'd dodged the big one. With everything else going on, I didn't need detention added to it.

Coach Dean kept Zander longer while I went ahead to my class, nicely preventing us from trying to skip out again. I had to hand it to him. He wasn't stupid.

In drama, my poor excuse about helping a teacher during lunch did not seem to suit Isaac, who glowered at me through most of class. I lost the courage to tell him I wanted to talk. He was already upset, so why make it worse?

Although Zander sat next to me in English, a pop quiz prevented him from saying anything to me, and as soon as class was over, Zena stalled him. Jealousy had my blood percolating. I left the room in a huff even though Zander made desperate eyes at me.

I chided myself later as I sat on a bench waiting for Dad. He should have been there already, so I turned on my phone to check for messages. Sure enough, he had left one indicating that there had been an emergency at work and he could not pick me up. He said I should wait with Ruthie at football practice and catch a ride. I so did not want to do that. Most of the players were, well, players and idiots. But I didn't have a choice, so I headed over toward the football field, texting Ruthie that I was coming with her after all.

"Tru!" A car crawled alongside me. I looked up to see Bobby in the passenger seat.

"Hi, Bobby." I smiled.

"Need a ride? I saw Ruthie at the field and she doesn't seem to be leaving any time soon."

I laughed. "No. That she is not. And my dad just bailed on me." I peered over at the driver. It was Dante, the strange kid who called me a dummy. I had passed him a few times in the hall since then, and each time, I felt uncomfortable.

Bobby hung an arm out the window and waved me over. "We can give you a ride, right, Dante?" He looked quickly at Dante, who gave me a toothy grin.

"Sure," Dante said.

"Uh, I don't know. My dad thinks I'm going home with Ruthie..." For some reason, I didn't feel right about going with them.

Bobby opened his door and walked up, grabbing my backpack. "Come on," he urged. "Shrina's coming, too." He looked back up the sidewalk. "And here she comes."

Sure enough, Shrina headed toward us, swinging her long black hair behind her. I bit my lip, considering Bobby's offer. I was just being silly. And I didn't want to wait for Ruthie, that's for sure.

"Hi, Tru!" said Shrina. "You coming with us?"

I shrugged. "Guess so."

Bobby smiled at us both. "Your carriage awaits you," he said, swinging open the car doors and grandly waving us in. We giggled. He placed both Shrina's backpack and mine in the trunk, and we headed off.

"So," I said once we were on our way, "thanks for giving me a ride, Dante. I hope it's not too far out of your way."

Dante had not contributed anything to the conversation thus far. He seemed deep in thought.

After a long pause, Bobby smacked him in the shoulder. "Hey, man, Tru's talking to you!" He swiveled around to me. "Sometimes he gets caught up in lyric land. It's not far out of our way, right, Dante?"

Dante met my gaze in the rearview mirror. His dark brown eyes seemed to come to a decision.

"It's not a problem," he said.

There was an awkward silence, during which Shrina mimed something that suggested *He's whacked!* I tucked in my lips, trying to prevent an all-out grin at her antics.

"Well, thanks anyway," I repeated.

Bobby reached over to find a song on the radio. "Dude! This song rocks!"

While the boys discussed the best radio stations, Shrina turned in her seat. "Hey," she pursed her lips conspiratorially. "You and Hottie Efoti, huh?"

She was just as bad as Ruthie with her need for details about everyone else's love life. I suppressed my annoyance and tried to derail her.

"Maybe... What's up with you and Bobby?"

Shrina's eyes widened, and I saw a flush run up her brown skin. She shook her head and I got the message. "Got it," I whispered.

Bobby turned around. "What are you guys whispering about?" He smiled. "Any good gossip?"

Shrina suavely waved him off. "Oh, we were just talking about who everyone is going to Homecoming with, that's all."

Bobby looked taken aback. "Really? Do you have a date already?" He almost seemed upset.

I sneaked a peek at Shrina. She shrugged. "Not yet, but rumors are afloat."

Oh, she was good. Bobby was eating this up, hook, line, and sinker. He turned back to the front. I gave Shrina a mental high-five, which she apparently understood because she winked at me.

Shrina was the first stop. She gave me a hug as she left. We were suddenly friends. I wore a happy grin as we pulled away from her house.

It occurred to me that I didn't know where Bobby lived, and I wondered if Dante was dropping him off before me. That would be really awkward. Just then, Bobby asked for directions. Apparently, he already knew the general area of my house.

As we approached the street that led to my neighborhood, Bobby suddenly slumped over.

"Hey, Bobby! Are you all right?" I reached over the seat to jostle his shoulder. "Oh my gosh! Dante, pull over!" I ripped off my seat belt and leaned partway over the seat to get a better look at Bobby.

Dante laughed. I looked at him in shock. What kind of game was he playing?

"Don't worry, Tru," he said. "Bobby is just sleeping. I bet you're sleepy, too." He grinned at me and reached his hand over to my arm.

What the heck? I thought.

"Yeah," he went on, "I think you need a nap, Tru."

Then everything went dark.

23

GOTCHA

I AWOKE TO THE smell of pine and ashes—and the mother of all headaches. I tried to bring my hands to my head, but they were being held in place. I opened my eyes to find my wrists tied with rope to the leg of a wooden chair. I yanked uselessly. What the...? Where was I? Blinking back my confusion, I sat up to assess my surroundings.

The small room couldn't have been more than twenty or thirty feet. The ceiling was made of bare, wooden beams, the walls knotty wood planks. Across the room stood a brown sofa with an end table and lamp. The sound of running water slipped out the bottom of a door next to it. My breath hitched. Who was that? A few scenes from different horror movies crossed my mind as I sped up my perusal of the room, looking for escape routes or possible weapons. Off to my right lay a small, faded kitchen with an old refrigerator, microwave, and sink. Rustic cupboards hung above a short counter. On the other side of me sat a woodstove. The door to this cozy establishment must be the large door not far from me with the lock on it. Two curtained windows nestled the door between them.

Clarity returned with a frame-by-frame replay of my car ride home after school. I recalled being in the car with Bobby and Dante. I remembered Bobby slumped over and Dante saying something about a nap.

How long had it been since then? I needed to get out of here before Dante, presumably the one on the other side of the door, returned. I could kill myself for not listening to that little voice that said "Don't get into the car with that weird kid." If I didn't do something now, someone else might take care of that for me.

I stood up carefully, bent over awkwardly since I had very little lag in the rope between my hands and the chair leg. I had to get to the door. The chair was pretty heavy, but I lifted it anyway and began to tiptoe to the door, praying that the wood floor wouldn't creak. Light as a feather, light as a feather.

No such luck. Due to the heavy chair, each step triggered a loud groan. Oh, for the love of… I decided to just make a break for it. At least I had a heavy weapon in my hands.

Just as I set the chair down to open the front door, the other door swung in, eliciting a squeak of the hinges. Dante stepped out of what appeared to be the bathroom, drying his hands on a towel.

I picked up the chair again, holding it in front of me defensively.

He laughed. "Tru. You aren't going anywhere. You don't even know where you are."

"My guess is that anywhere else is better than here."

"Not necessarily. Besides, you wouldn't make it two steps before I caught you, and then what would you do?"

He walked slowly toward me. In this setting I realized he was not a teenager. He was definitely not a high school student. He was taller than me and lean, with veiny muscle. I didn't doubt that he could catch up to me.

I raised the chair. It felt amazingly light all of a sudden. "Don't come any closer."

He rolled his eyes. "Really? You think I can't fend off a little girl holding a chair?"

"You can try," I stated bravely.

"Fine. Go ahead. Open the door. You'll find yourself surrounded by miles and miles of forest. You won't make it very far, so maybe you will be served best conserving your strength for the moment. Right now, I just want to talk with you. Promise." He held up his hands innocently, like he wasn't some psychopath who had kidnapped me and done who knows what to Bobby.

"Where's Bobby?"

"Don't worry about him. I dropped him off at some park. He'll get home fine when he wakes up. He's probably already home."

I hoped he called to check on me. Would he keep trying to find me or tell my dad I was missing? Did he know I was missing? I decided to look outside to see if Dante was bluffing. I had to set down my only weapon to do it, but Dante stayed where he was. I picked up the chair again and walked out, closing the door behind me. Sure enough, there were trees as far as I could see. Towering Douglas firs and redwoods, as well as miles and miles of ferns and poison oak. Still, it seemed more inviting than the cabin. The trees blocked out most of the sun, but I could see it breaking through the branches. It seemed like the middle of the afternoon. His car sat off to the side, under a makeshift carport. A rutty-looking road, barely wide enough for a car, curved around the trees and out of sight.

Would he let me keep walking? I doubted it. How far could I carry this stupid chair? Maybe I could surprise him when he followed me out.

I stepped to the side of the door and held the chair up so I could swing it at him when he stepped out of the door.

I could hear the stupid floorboards creaking as he walked across them. I tensed, ready to bring him down. Part of my brain knew I was hopped up on adrenaline, and I encouraged the self-preserving madness of this violent side of me. I imagined the chair breaking his face.

"I know you are standing by the door, Tru. I'm not an idiot. Besides, I can see you in the window." Dante's muffled voice easily penetrated the door.

Ugh! I forgot the windows.

"We can wait all day, if you want," he continued. "Or you can just come in here and find out who you really are and why you can do what you do."

Who you really are? Why you can do what you do?

The words ricocheted around my skull, and all at once I couldn't hold up the chair any longer.

He had answers to questions I hadn't quite given life to, but suddenly needed to know, desperately.

The door swung open wide. I stepped in front of it. He stood to the side, one hand out, inviting me in like a long-awaited guest.

I picked up my burden and followed it into his irresistible trap.

24

Rainbows and Unicorns

"Okay, start talking."

Dante had kindly untied me long enough to use the bathroom, in which I had found nothing remotely useful as a weapon other than shampoo and soap. I imagined squirting the soap all over the floor and him slipping on it and breaking his neck, which kind of made me feel a little better. But eventually I returned to the room, where he politely held out the chair for me to seat myself before retying one wrist to the back of it. My wrist was already turning red.

"I'm not sure where to start, honestly." He leaned back into the sofa, a thin laptop next to him.

"What did you mean by *who I really am?*"

"I told you at school. You are idimmu." He smirked.

I thought he had called me a dummy. "Yeah, what's that?"

"That's your *true nature.* Not human like you've been pretending to be so far. Time to embrace it, girl."

"But what's the difference between humans and idimmu?"

"The difference is ordinary—" He held up one palm. "And extraordinary." He raised the other. "It's awesome! We've been called many names, though—witches, warlocks, fae, sirens, half-breeds, demons, the list goes on. Sometimes it depends on what you can do. In general, all idimmu are *gifted.*"

"You left out unicorns." I rolled my eyes.

He laughed. "They would be cool, right?"

Exasperated, I tried again. "Look, I think you've got the wrong person."

No way was I any of those crazy things. I just had better eyesight than most. Nowhere in that list was werewolf, which was the only mystical being in my life right now. Of course, I had no proof yet. Man! I should have made a run for it after all. I wondered if Zander had called me. Where was my phone anyway? In my backpack, of course, which was probably still in the car.

Dante stood up and walked over to the refrigerator.

"Oh, really? I saw what you did for Bobby, you know." He pulled out a soda, extending it out to me like we were friends just hanging out. I shook my head even though my mouth was as dry as the dirt road outside. He shrugged and popped the can open before sitting back down on the sofa. He took a swig and let out a deep, satisfied breath.

"That's my gift, by the way," he added.

I was having a hard time keeping up. "What?"

"I can see auras and, baby, yours lit up like a rainbow when you talked to Bobby that first day!"

I gave him my best you-are-a-whacko look.

"Sure, it may not be your average superhero power, but it's very useful to the folks in charge. I'm just doing what I have to do to survive. You'd do the same thing."

Dante's voice raised and his eyes got a little crazy, like he was going to snap any minute. Dang! What was in that drink? Looked like your average soda, which meant he had a few more screws loose than I originally thought.

"Whoa, there. Auras. No, I think that would be way cool." I had to calm him down. Uber-polite Dante was way better than hanging-by-a-thread Dante. He ran a hand over his face, pausing as if fighting for control.

"And like every superhero, we have a weakness," he continued. He opened his eyes, and they looked sad, yet resigned somehow.

"We all have the same weakness?" For some reason, I felt like he was being straight with me.

"Yeah. Afraid so."

"Then what is it?" I whispered. Somehow, I knew what he was going to say. No. No. No!

"Eventually, we all go insane."

There. He said it. I *was* a psycho. I could feel the truth of his words. I'd rather die than go insane.

"Is there a cure?" My voice wobbled.

"No. Afraid not. But there used to be a certain individual who could temper it, kind of take the edge off, so to speak. Unfortunately, she ran away."

"She?"

"Yeah, some usemi they captured a long time ago. I don't know much about her."

"Usemi?" Peter and Zander's conversation about my mother's accident came to mind. They said a usemi was involved in the accident.

"Man, I could use a white board right now." Dante laughed. "Actually," he continued, "I should just show you my secret website. The people I work for are not the most honorable, if you know what I mean. I've been saving information about them and all kinds of stuff, including whatever histories I can find about us, usemi, akharu, the sethians, and all that crap, just in case I need blackmail material. Man, I've got quite a collection, which is totally ironic because they call my boss 'the Collector.' He collects us, uses our gifts for his projects." He sighed as if to say, *Oh well* and stared out the window thoughtfully.

Too much information and not enough, all at the same time. I needed to narrow it down.

"Look, Dante," I said, leaning forward. "I want to know more about idimmu, usemi, and akharu." I stumbled over the new words. "Can you tell me about them?"

"Sure. Why not? You're going to see it all up close and personal soon enough."

I tamped down the fear bubbling up. One problem at a time. "Go on," I urged.

"Here, let me bring up my website for you. It's not published yet. I'm going to rig it to go public if I don't enter my password periodically. Unfortunately, the Internet is really spotty out here. I have to go into town to publish it. It's going to be amazing!" He scooted to the end of the sofa, close to my chair, with his laptop out. I peered at the screen.

A Hello Kitty background popped up with a login box.

"Hello Kitty?"

He laughed gleefully. "I know, right? Who would guess that this site contains some of the biggest secrets in the world? Pink is so innocuous!"

I had to agree with him there. He started punching in a login name: ICANCU.

Before I thought better of it, I blurted out, "I. Can. See. You. You see auras. Good username."

Dante grinned, then frowned. "I know! You don't think it's too obvious, do you? Wait!" He turned the keyboard away from me to type in the password.

Fine, I thought. *Be secretive.*

When he swiveled back to me, sounds of sword fighting, growling, and screaming streamed from the speaker and then fell silent.

I smirked at him. “Really?”

He shrugged. “I get bored sometimes.”

He ran his fingers across the keys and up popped image after image of fanged beings, some human-looking and some wolf. They looked like some of the creatures in my dreams. How was my imagination conjuring up the same things that Dante had on his computer, beings he claimed were real? I had firsthand knowledge of the wolves, but did that mean everything else he said was also true? I was beginning to think crazy Dante was telling the truth about everything.

He pointed to a couple of wolves fighting. “Those are usemi. Also known as werewolves or lycans. There’s a lot of myth and lore about them, some true, some not. The bare bones version is that they are real, but very rare. I don’t know how far back they go, but I do know that their population has been dwindling. If humans knew of them, they’d put them on the endangered species list. Akharu, too.”

He pointed to another picture. A black-haired man with glowing red eyes bared his teeth ferociously. His shoulders were wide and curved, his fingers curled. He looked like a cross between a big hissing cat at the zoo and a lean version of the Incredible Hulk, except he wasn’t green.

"That's Donavitch, also known to many as son of a—"

"I get it, thanks."

"Well. No one messes with him to his face."

"How did you get these pictures?"

"Oh, from the different Nasaru bases around the world. Nasaru is kind of the ruling party for all these creatures, really old, run by sethians, the third ancient purebred. The purebreds include sethian, usemi, and akharu."

He pointed to a human-looking soldier.

"He's a sethian. They don't change into animals, drink blood, or have gifts like you or I—well, I take that back. Those closest to the top have found a way to do different mind-controlling tricks. They say they've been blessed. But I have a different theory about that."

He dismissed it with a wave. "Their tricks are only temporary. The strongest one is the Collector, of course. Not many folks know him as that. It's kind of his secret side job. His main job is to run the Nasaru, kind of like their king or president. They call him *Malku.* It means 'prince.' Sometimes they call him *Malku Kasadu,* which means 'the prince who overcomes.' He's their big hope for a brighter future, blah, blah, blah. Unless you were raised with them, it sounds very cult-like, I know."

"This place doesn't sound very nice. Why do you stay with them?"

He sighed. "I know, right? Like I said. Self-preservation. Once you are 'collected,' you don't get to leave. But I'm different. I am allowed to leave because I find more idimmu for him."

"But why go back? You're free now."

"Not really. Remember what I said about our weakness? It started years ago for me. I thought it was schizophrenia at first, but then they took me to see this usemi and she fixed me, although I was really freaked out because she seemed a little crazy herself. But I kept going back because I needed to be fixed now and then. It's been a long time, though, and now she's run away... I think they had her fix too many people and it broke her. "

"So usemi and akharu have special gifts, too?"

"Oh, no, not like that. Usemi are super strong and live a really, really long time. They are hard to kill, but they aren't immortal. They heal faster than humans, but they are definitely nothing like the creatures you see in the movies. They retain all their faculties when they change. And they don't go around killing and eating humans." He laughed.

"Well, that's good."

"Sure. If they did, you'd be hearing a lot more about them. Anyway, akharu, or vampires, are super smart and live a long time, too. Again, not immortal. When I say super smart, I mean that their brains are wired differently, or maybe they just use more of their brains. I don't know for sure. But they're creepy in their own right. It's like they know what you're going to say or do before you do it because they've thought through all the possible scenarios in their minds, factored in all the minute personality traits they know about you, all the visual clues, and the immediate circumstances, and make the best educated prediction regarding what you'll say or do. It's a little like being around one of those autistic kids who can do intricate calculations in their heads, but akharu don't have all the social problems autistics have, if you know what I mean. At least that's what most people say. I beg to differ, though, because the couple I've met annoyed the hell out of me. They can be the most pretentious snobs. They usually keep to themselves, you know, too good for the rest of us folks."

"Wow. They sound lovely." I hoped to never meet one.

"Yeah. Fortunately, there aren't many left. Like I said, usemi and akharu are dying out."

"So, can they do weird stuff like you?"

"No. They don't have gifts like *us*." He smirked.

While I was starting to believe all this crazy stuff, I was still in denial about where I fit into the picture.

"But you said a usemi fixed you."

"Yeah, but this particular usemi is unusual. I heard she was originally idimmu and got turned by a usemi. She's the only known case of it."

"What do you mean? I thought that's how one became a werewolf—you know, a bite or a scratch?"

He laughed. "Like I said, myth and lore. Usemi and akharu are born, not made. Remember I said they were going extinct? Usemi and akharu can only have offspring with their mates, as in the only other living creature they can truly love and procreate with."

"But how did she become usemi then?"

"That's a bit of a mystery. I think the Collector knows. There are lots of rumors, though. Some say that the Collector experimented on her—he's got a lot of really sketchy stuff going on in his laboratories. My favorite story is that she was bitten by her true mate, and their love was so strong that she survived the change."

"Wait, you said people couldn't be turned into usemi!"

"Yeah, because usemi bites are poison to humans. They die within days. Plus, it's illegal. That's one of the jobs of a sethian, to enforce the laws of the purebreds."

"Okay. So you think her true mate bit her?" This sad story gave me a brain itch, a Ruthie-ism for times when you knew you should remember something but couldn't put the pieces together.

"Possibly, although if he did, he's probably dead now because true mates can't be apart very long. And also, she had an illegal kid with an akharu. Heard he died when she was captured."

Oh my gosh! I remembered the last dream I'd shared with Ruthie, the one about the good-looking Euro vampire and the wolf.

"I know, seriously sad and messed up," he continued, although I was barely listening.

"Some say the usemi and akharu are descendants of Cain and Abel and that they were cursed to be what they are now. There are lots of theories regarding the curses, but that's neither here nor there."

Here nor there? Who says that? I thought. My head was busting with new information, old dreams involving biblical characters, and what this meant for me. I still didn't understand how I fit into things.

"What about the sethians? What's their thing? You said some have superpowers. Do they live long, too? And when you say a long time, just how long are we talking?" The picture of the soldier still displayed on Dante's computer screen. He looked human, like any modern-day soldier. He wore fatigues and carried a gun. Other instruments were clipped to his waist.

"Well, I've heard that sethians used to live just as long as usemi and akharu, but many, many years ago their life spans began shortening until now they live as long as humans. I've also heard that there are still sethians out there who have retained their longevity, something about them remaining uncorrupted. But I'm not sure what that means. Anyway, you remember the Bible characters like Noah and Methuselah? They were sethian and they lived almost a thousand years."

"Wow." My fall-asleep-faster tactic, reading the Bible, just got more interesting. I was definitely going to look up these sethians—if I ever got away from Dante.

"And their powers?" I prompted.

"Oh, no. No powers, except for the uppity-ups. But they aren't like ours. They seem to weaken over time, so they have to reinforce them."

I was curious. "What do you mean?"

"Well, the official story is that they have some kind of secret ceremony during which the Great Spirit blesses them with gifts to help them strengthen the sethians as a whole, enforce the laws over the other races, and protect humans." Dante's face was skeptical.

"But you don't believe it?" I asked.

"Let's just say I think the Collector collects idimmu for more than their gifts—Oh, I shouldn't have told you that."

A cold finger ran up my spine. "Dante, what does he really do with them."

Dante stood up quickly and headed to the small kitchen. He crushed his empty soda can in his hand before tossing it in a trashcan.

"You know, it doesn't really matter. Nothing you or I can do about it anyway." He picked up his phone to check his messages.

He wasn't going to tell me any more about it. So I took a different approach. "Dante, I thought you said the usemi that fixed you ran away. Why would you go back now?"

He turned his full gaze on me then, and his eyes were wild again. A creepy smile spread across his face as he tilted his head mockingly.

"Why, Tru! I thought it would be obvious! I have you now. You can be the new fixer. The Collector is going to be so happy with me. He hoped that I would find Dubois, but I think I found something better!" He almost cackled.

Throughout his psychotic self-congratulations, two things stood out. One, he thought what I did for Bobby made me like whoever fixed him, and two, I'd heard the name Dubois before. It certainly wasn't a common name. Zander and Peter referred to my wolf as Dubois. Everything seemed connected, but I couldn't piece it all together yet. I felt dizzy and betrayed. I thought Dante was coming around. He seemed so normal most of the time. But now I realized that he truly was crazy.

Refocusing on my surroundings, I saw that Dante had pulled away a rug in front of the sofa and flipped open a trapdoor in the floor.

"No! You have it all wrong!" I couldn't fix people like he thought. I just knew how to be nice. I wasn't gifted. I was just a dumb girl who should have run when she had the chance.

Dante stood behind my chair, tipping it slightly to make me stand.

"Sorry, Tru, but it's true!" He giggled. "Did I ever tell you I liked your name?"

"Dante!" I leaned hard backward, desperate—desperate enough to turn in my wolf. "What if I said I knew where the Fixer was?"

He laughed hard now. "Oh, come on! I have a feeling you would say just about anything right now."

There was no way I was going down into that dark hole without a fight. I rolled out of my chair, picking it up to swing at him, but he grabbed it before I could build up any momentum. His eyes glinted with fury and he growled through clenched teeth.

"I was going to untie you first, but have it your way!"

25

Pitiful

With one shove I was weightless seconds before falling through a dark hole and landing so very, very wrong, one ankle folding like a napkin, causing me to wrench back, smacking an elbow on the cement floor. The heavy wooden chair landed and broke beside me, but not before smacking me in the hip. My elbow throbbed. It was the mother of all funny bone injuries. I felt sure that my arm was never going to straighten again and that a bone may have penetrated my skin. The pain stole my breath far too long, and then I was gasping and coughing from lack of air and excruciating agony. I tried not to move, because the tiniest shift in my position made the contents of my stomach rise up.

"Oh, dear," said a sickly sweet voice above me. Light from the room above surrounded me. Looking up, I could see Dante's dark silhouette. "Did you hurt yourself?" He mocked. "Sorry about that. At least it will keep you from trying to escape. Oh, right! You can heal yourself! So what's that saying? *Physician, heal thyself?* That's it." He pulled out his cell phone and tapped it.

"I don't know how, you idiot!" I screamed. With pain shooting through my entire body, my voice came out sounding as crazy as his. It was like I'd been transported to someone else's nightmare, too horrible to be happening to me. Slowly, the initial shards of agony faded into a layer of numbness that allowed me to lie back on the ground.

Dante squatted, a dark silhouette in the cellar doorway. He sighed dramatically. "Tru, Tru, Tru. You do, too. I saw you, you little liar." He paused and squeezed his head with both hands. "As you can see, I'm not quite myself. So the sooner we get you to the Collector, the sooner I can be fixed." He spoke sweetly, like he was talking to a little child.

"Then why didn't you have me fix you before you shoved me down here!"

"Tut, tut, Tru—oh my, the alliteration! It's lovely, isn't it?" He repeated the words several times, smiling. "Dear, sweet, girl. Your talent could go both ways. How can I trust you to fix me instead of breaking me more? No, no, I need the Collector to make you fix me. He has ways to make people do what he wants."

A hopeless sob escaped me.

"There, there now. Don't worry. All will be well. I think you are going to make me very rich, sweetheart, yes I do." The more he spoke, the more song-like his voice became.

"They're going to realize I'm missing," I bit out with a low growl, grinding my teeth. I had to stop talking, or I'd really vomit, and that would make my misery so much worse. Cold sweat had broken out over my lip. Dante still heard me.

"I suppose. But they won't find you in time. Those brothers! The Collector really has silly sons. Oh! Alliteration again. Did you hear it? Silly sons. Silly sons."

"What?" Who was he talking about now? I suspected, but didn't want to believe it.

"Zander and Peter, of course! Although, they have no idea who the Collector is." He cackled. "What? Did you really think Zander liked you? Stupid girl. He was looking for the same thing I was! But I figured it out first!"

Suddenly, Dante grabbed his head like he was going to smash it between his palms. He yelled, "Stop it. Stop it!" And then he lay on the ground next to the opening. He must have passed out.

I wanted to scream out loud, but kept it in my head. Zander really was using me all along. It felt like little blood vessels around my heart were popping. Maybe this was what it felt like to get your heart broken. But to do so, you had to love someone first. Did I love him? It didn't matter anymore. Zander wasn't coming to help me. But someone would, right?

Someone, please help me! I sent my plea out into the universe. No one knew where I was. Would Ruthie or Isaac look for me?

Above me, Dante groaned. He rolled over and looked down at me.

"Tru? What are you doing down there?"

"Are you serious?"

His eyebrows turned down at the corners. "Oh, man! I'm sorry about this. I must have lost it there for a while."

Relief poured back into my chest and I breathed a little easier. "Ha ha. Can you help me out of here?"

"Actually, you are right where you need to be for now. I just didn't mean to hurt you. So sorry! But don't worry, I'll get someone to come pick us up ASAP."

He started humming as he tapped away on his phone.

What? I couldn't keep up with his personalities. I started shivering. It wasn't that cold down here. I must be going into shock. I was going to die in a cellar, in a pit of no mercy, in the middle of nowhere, and my friends and family would never know what happened to me. I allowed the tears to fall.

Dante moved his phone around in the air, whispering something about service.

"Hey, are you okay down there?"

I opened my eyes. He was looking down at me, but all I could see was his silhouette.

"There should be a sleeping bag somewhere around there. Oh, I'm sure you can figure it out."

I still didn't say anything. It hurt to talk. I thought of Ruthie and how kick-butt she was. Really. She didn't seem like the type, but she took martial arts classes with her brothers and could really tear someone up if needed. I smiled just thinking of her.

I breathed in and out, trying to manage my panic. I was not dead yet. Slowly but surely, my shivers died down. I was positive my ankle was broken. For once, I was grateful for the ability to see in the dark. I could even make out the walls around me. Shelves lined them, stuffed with boxes. I was beginning to suspect this was one of those underground survival hideaways. Perhaps there was a weapon or something in those boxes that I could use to get out of here. I needed to scoot over there. Plus, I hated that he could see me so clearly while he remained a black outline above. I took a look at the chair I was shackled to and received my first bit of good luck. It had broken, and with a painful yank and wiggle, I slipped the knotted rope from the chair's thick spindle. I bit my lips as I tried to drag myself toward the shelves. I only made it to the edge of the light before coming to a gasping stop. At least he couldn't see my face anymore. No, I'd make it to those stupid shelves and find something to help me.

Crazy must have been reading my mind.

"You know? You remind me of a cockroach scurrying to a dark corner." He chuckled. "Just to save you the effort, I removed the ladders and guns and pretty much anything you might be hoping to find." He disappeared for a second and was back with a flashlight. I lifted a hand to block the beam of light shining into my face.

"There you are, sweetheart!" He turned off the light. "Just checking on you. I'll come down later, when I bring your dinner. I can't have you fading away on me. Besides, we could get to know each other better, no?"

He started to disappear again, and despite my awful fear of him, I was more afraid of him making that phone call. Right now, my best friend's name was Stall.

"Wait!" I called.

He paused and squatted back down.

"Aw, you missed me already?" He turned off the flashlight and set it on the floor next to him.

"Tell me more about what I am."

He had called it my "true nature" before. I'd always thought that referred to the type of person you were, not what kind of being you were. Did an animal act solely based on its biological makeup or on something else I couldn't name, maybe its soul? Personality? Was it a mix of them all? Was a being's true nature a combination of all these things? It didn't seem fair to lump a person's true nature in one category. To me, the true nature of a being was as unique as a fingerprint.

"Sure, Tru. I wonder which one it is? Your father or mother?"

"What about them?"

"Was it your father or mother that spawned you? You know, which one of them was akharu or usemi?"

"Easy. Neither." What was he talking about?

Dante tilted his head back and cawed loudly. "You really don't know, do you? Did I forget to mention how we become idimmu?" He was back to his singsong voice.

"Yeah. That seems kind of important to know."

"Well, sweetheart, I hate to break it to you this way, but one of your parents has to be akharu—aka vampire or blood-sucking spawns of Cain—or usemi—aka lycanthrope or Abel's cursed descendants. My father was usemi, or so the Collector told me. He can do a blood test and find out. The bastard left my mother when I was just a baby. Usemi are natural wanderers, like gypsies."

My mind swirled at his words. How was this possible? How could my parents hide this from me? No, there was no proof. Seeing in the dark didn't prove anything. But Dante was definitely a demon in my book.

"I know it's a bit of a shock and all, and I'm sure your parents are nice folks, but one of them caused this. It's not your fault. They broke the law, not you. It is unfortunate that we have to pay the price, though. We are twice cursed creatures.

"Remember me saying that some call us half-breeds or demons? Sethians are afraid of what we can do. They convinced everyone that we need to be locked up—or worse—to protect good folks everywhere. Sure, some of us are dangerous, but every race has its psychopaths."

"Who thinks we need to be locked up?"

"The pure races, of course—sethians, akharu, usemi. Well, probably not our parents, but the rest of them. It's always about power, and baby, we have power. Now if we could just stay sane long enough to overthrow them, yeah, that would change the world, wouldn't it?"

My thoughts exactly. Anyone who controlled the idimmu would have a lot of power. No wonder they wanted a healer.

"What exactly can you do again?" I asked.

"I told you! I see auras. Different kinds of creatures have different auras, and you have the most colors I've ever seen. Odd that yours are so different from our last healer. But that must be because she was also usemi. Yeah, that must be it."

"But you can do more, can't you? You made Bobby and me go to sleep with just a touch, didn't you?" It seemed so strange, but I had recently seen werewolves in my backyard and a mind-erasing army guy.

"Yes. They call me the Sandman. Isn't that clever? It's way more humane than other forms of fighting, don't you think?" He yawned loudly. He was getting tired of this conversation.

"How do you know someone is, uh, idimmu? I mean, how does their aura look?" I asked instead.

"Well, their aura changes when they use their gift. Usually, people have one strong color tinged with other colors depending on their mood. When idimmu use their gifts, they become multicolored, usually two or three dominant colors, and their pattern is different than a human's."

"What color am I?"

"You? As far as I remember, you are every color."

"What do you mean? I thought idimmu had just a few colors."

"I know!" He seemed excited. "That's what I mean. Your aura is beautiful! It's like a shimmery spectrum that goes on and on. The most powerful idimmu I saw before you had four colors."

Well, that sounded pretty weird. I was a freaking rainbow. Bring on the leprechauns.

"And," he continued, "when you helped Bobby at lunch the other day, your aura was so bright, I had to shield my eyes! I knew you were doing something to him. I think you fixed his head, you know, his depression."

That wasn't possible. Suddenly, I didn't want to know any more. Perhaps whatever Dante had was contagious. I was beginning to believe the mad ravings of a lunatic. But was I really any different than before? I mean, just last year I was a walking coma. If I was this "idimmu" that Dante was going on about, then my stint with insanity could have been the beginning of more. Would I end up like him?

"Dante, I think I need a doctor."

"What? You haven't fixed yourself yet? Oh, well. No worries. When I call this in, they'll send one to help you."

Panic enveloped me again. I didn't want to be collected. That sounded very, very bad.

"Dante, please! My dad needs me." I couldn't leave him like Mom left us. It would be worse, because I would simply disappear. I'd become some picture on a milk carton.

"You think someone didn't need me?" He was angry now. He stood up suddenly and slammed the door shut. Tears dripped down my face, onto the gritty floor. Strangely, only one person's face flitted through my mind. It wasn't family. It wasn't my best friend. It was Zander, even if he was the son of the Collector. Looked like I might be the daughter of a werewolf or vampire. That didn't make me bad, did it? I wondered if I would ever see him again.

26

Revelation

THANKS TO MY NIGHT vision, I could easily locate the sleeping bag. It smelled like it had been down there for 50 years, but it was warmer than the stone floor. I climbed in as best as I could, the pain exhausting me by the time I finished. Without meaning to, I closed my eyes and let reality slip away.

Ruthie screamed near the school parking lot.

"Tru Lee Parker! You better get your butt over here right now!"

Phoebe snickered next to her. "Is that seriously her middle name?"

Impatiently, Ruthie snapped back, "Why would I make up a name like that? Where is she?" She glanced at her cell phone. "She didn't text me and she isn't answering her phone. I'm supposed to meet Val at Yogurt Heaven in thirty minutes!"

"So that's why you're so grumpy."

Ruthie just glared at her, hands on her hips.

Phoebe defended herself. "Hey, it's not my fault! Isaac has been looking for her for the past hour. He's been all over the school and even went by her house. Says he can't smell—I mean, he hasn't seen her anywhere."

"Great!" Ruthie said.

It took me longer to figure out that this was a dream because it felt so real and I had just been there a few hours ago. I'd never dreamed about something so recent. I had begun to suspect during my conversations with Dante that my strange dreams were of actual events, not figments of my overactive imagination. That meant Ruthie was finished watching Val's practice and someone was finally noticing that I was missing—at least I hoped.

"Do you think she would have left school with someone else?" Phoebe asked.

Ruthie paused, one side of her mouth turned down. "She wouldn't!" she mumbled. I could tell she was wondering if I had gone with Zander. She turned to Phoebe. "Well..."

Don't say it, I thought. As if I had any control here.

Phoebe raised her eyebrows, waiting. Finally, Ruthie shook her head. "No, I don't think so. She would have texted me if she did."

"Is something going on that you want to share with me?" asked Phoebe.

"Uh, no, really," insisted Ruthie. "I'm actually starting to get a little worried now."

"Maybe we should call her dad."

"Oh my gosh. I don't think I have his cell number. Tru said he was working late tonight. I should call my mom." Ruthie punched into her phone.

The scene shifted.

Zander was talking with his brother in front of a hotel. He suddenly threw up his hands and took off down the road. When he was far enough away from his brother, he slipped into the trees alongside the road and took off running, fast. From my strange vantage point, I could see that he was moving faster than the cars parallel to him on the other side of the trees. He slowed down whenever he had to come out in the open, but speeded up within the protection of the trees. Then, he was sneaking into my house. Then he was slipping back out, his face tightened in frustration.

Next, I saw him at my recreation center, then back at the school.

Hope lit up my insides. He seemed to care. Maybe Dante had it all wrong.

Zander paced aimlessly in front of the empty school. The sun was disappearing behind the thickly forested hillside. Suddenly he grabbed a large rock from the side of the parking lot and hurled it into the trees. But the trees were a hundred yards away, and the rock embedded itself into the trunk of a large pine tree, which shook from the impact, needles and pinecones dropping.

His phone started ringing. He checked the caller and then answered.

"I can't find her."

"Yes, I checked everywhere."

"What did you find out?"

"Ancient prophecy?"

Zander started pacing again, and ran his hand through his hair, leaving it sticking up.

"How do I feel? What do you mean? I'm freaking out!"

"Normal? Are you kidding me? I don't know why, I just feel like she's in danger. I can't explain it."

"If you think this will help me find her—"

"Okay. Since the first day of school, no, since I got here. Actually, I think I've been feeling it forever, but more after about a year ago."

"Yeah. About the same time as the accident."

"Strange coincidence? Where are you going with this?"

"Sword of what? Shield of Arammusatu? Is that what I think it is? Are you freaking kidding me? Not the same?"

"Forget it. Just tell me how this helps Tru!"

Zander sank down to the curb.

"Does this mean she isn't a siren?"

"Yeah, that would explain how I've been feeling. I mean, it actually hurts to stay away from her. And she doesn't look too good either."

"I don't know, I've been trying so hard to ignore it..."

"How do I do it?"

"Conrad, I'm not going to sit yoga style. And 'no' to the spa music, too." He blew out an exasperated breath. "Fine! Hold on a second. I'm going to put the phone down for a minute. But no music."

He walked around the side of a building and sat cross-legged, placing his hands on his knees. He rolled his shoulders and took a few deep breaths. Seconds rolled by.

Suddenly he cried out in pain, grabbing his ankle. Then he grabbed his arm, holding it carefully.

"What the—"

A loud, yet indistinguishable voice yelled out of the phone. Zander gingerly reached out with his good arm and hit the speaker button.

"—Zander! What's happening! Should I call someone?"

"No, Conrad. But I don't know what's going on. I tried to meditate just like you said and feel that 'pull' to Tru like I described to you, and just when I felt like I connected, I started hurting all over. It feels like my ankle is broken, and maybe my arm, too. But everything looks normal."

"That's good," replied Conrad. "I mean that's not good, but I think you connected to her. The bad news is that if you are, then you are probably feeling what she feels, which means she's injured. The good news is that you aren't messed up and you should be able to power through the pain and move normally. Just imagine that 'pull' as a thick thread and follow it. It should lead you right to her."

Zander's face had hardened during Conrad's explanation. When he looked up to the road, his eyes blazed deep blue, like ultraviolet light.

"Thanks, Conrad." Zander looked like he wanted to kill something. "I'll get back to you later."

"Good luck, Z."

Zander stashed his phone and took off running.

Steps across the creaking floorboards woke me. Wow. That dream! Was it real? Or did I just want it to be?

I wondered how late it was, how long I'd been down here in this pit. Then I heard someone calling out. I listened more carefully.

"Tru!"

That wasn't Dante.

"Tru!"

The rug was lifted from the trapdoor and light filtered in around the edges.

"Zander?" My voice was croaky. I tried again. "Zander!"

The trapdoor opened and Zander's figure filled the entrance.

"Tru!"

"Zander!" I almost screamed.

"Shhhh!" Zander warned, speaking quickly. "I'm getting you out of here. Dante is outside talking on his phone. He's walking up the road to get better reception. But we have to hur—Wait! He's coming back. I'll take care of him first. Then I'll get you out."

"Don't let him touch you—" I said as he shut the door.

He hadn't let me finish warning him about Dante.

"Dang it!" I slammed the ground with my good fist. "Ow!"

27

Confessions

My heart contracted as I strained to hear something, anything. All I got was a muffled conversation. Had Zander heard me? He couldn't let Dante touch him! If he did, we were toast. I tried to shift directly under the opening, hoping for a better position to yell up at them, but realized it wasn't going to work. Out of breath, my injuries throbbing, I lay waiting.

Suddenly, the rug lifted, and light streaked across me, blinding me for a moment.

"Oh, Tru-u!"

I let out a disappointed whimper when I recognized the voice.

"You'll never believe it!" Dante giggled. "It's a two-fer! I think I'll take a cruise after this one!" His giggles became deeper, creepier.

What had he done with Zander?

"Honey, you might want to move out of the way."

I had just enough time to scoot over before a large shape landed next to me with a crack. I grimaced, certain that a bone had just broken.

Zander lay in a heap, both arms tied behind his back, and his feet tied together. I wasn't sure what was broken, but his shoulder looked really wrong.

"There you go. Please, no need to thank me." His face leaned into the hole, glee spreading his smile wide. "Someone to talk to. You're one lucky girl!

"Of course, I'm one lucky guy, as well! Perhaps I should take a closer look at all your friends, dearie. His aura is almost as beautiful as yours! Whatever you are, you two are amazingly similar. The Collector is going to be so happy! Of course there may be a little family drama for a bit, but I'm sure he'll be pleased just the same. I don't know how I never noticed him before!"

I stared at Zander. He was like me? I choked back a sob and scooted closer, ignoring my own pain. He looked broken. Anger swept through me like brush fire.

"Idiot!" I yelled. "You might have killed him. I think he broke something." Gritting my teeth against the pain from my ankle, I felt for his pulse. I sighed in relief when I picked up a strong beat.

"Oh, good! I was hoping he broke something." Dante's voice went up a couple of octaves. "I wouldn't want him trying to escape before your ride comes. Now sit tight. I need to run out to the road and make a call. Don't worry, I'll be back in just a few minutes." The trapdoor closed.

"Zander!" I had to wake him up. If we didn't want to be collected, we needed to get out of here before Dante came back. Yeah, it was a long shot, but Zander was bound to have an idea to get us out of here. And if that dream told me anything, it was that Zander had some secret abilities that would help.

"Zander!" I wrapped his face in my hands, shaking him gently. I wasn't sure what was broken, but I suspected he might have dislocated his shoulder.

He didn't budge. Whatever Dante did to him really knocked him out. I looked around the room again for anything to help me. A pack of water bottles sat on one of the shelves. I crawled across the floor, dragging my broken ankle, spewing as many Ruthie cusswords as I could remember. I pulled the bottles down and slowly made my way back. Pausing next to Zander, I carefully poked at my ankle only to find that it had been replaced by a grapefruit. I wondered if I should take off my shoe. No, I'd deal with it later.

Taking the lid off one of the bottles, I hung it over Zander's face. It seemed cruel to wake him up to what was sure to be excruciating pain. But, then again, if I didn't, we were definitely becoming museum pieces.

Biting my lip, I tipped the bottle, letting the water splash over his face.

He woke up sputtering, trying to move away from the water. But when he moved, he yelped. As sorry as I was that he was hurt and stuck down here with me, a thrill went through me, making me chuckle.

"Agh!" he moaned, trying to sit up, but it must have hurt too much because he let out a sharp gasp and lay back down. "That wasn't funny! What the hell happened?"

I realized suddenly that he couldn't see me. The room was completely dark.

"Zander! It's me. I'm here with you." I rested one hand on his chest gently, not sure where he hurt.

"Tru?" He was turned on his side because his hands were tied behind his back. "Oh hell, he got me, didn't he? Man! How?"

"Don't feel too badly. When he touches people, they pass out."

"I didn't see that one coming. You tried to warn me, didn't you?" He attempted to get up again, but fell back breathing hard.

"Don't move," I said. "I think you broke something when he dropped you down here."

"He dropped me through that hole? Is that how you hurt your ankle?"

My jaw dropped in shock. "How did you know I broke my ankle?" Even though I knew how from my dream, I hadn't quite connected it with reality. The fact that he was here should have proven to me the truth of what I had witnessed, but I couldn't quite make that leap yet.

He shook his head. "I don't know. Seriously, so many weird things have been happening to me today. I could just, I don't know, sense it, I suppose."

"I know."

"You know?"

"I mean, I've been learning so much suddenly, too. And then I dreamed that you were talking with your friend Conrad, and—"

"You dreamed that?"

"Yeah...weird, I know. It's almost too much to believe, but just before you opened the trapdoor, I woke up. In the dream you were at my house and at the school, searching for me, and then you could feel my pain... I know that sounds crazy...I'm afraid I might still be dreaming..."

Zander shook his head. "No. You're right! I know I have a lot of explaining to do. And I have a lot of questions for you. But first things first."

I knew he couldn't see me, but his face was turned toward me and it almost seemed like he was looking right at me. Tears were slipping down my cheeks and I was glad he couldn't see them.

"Tru," he continued, "I want you to know that you're important to me. I haven't been messing with you. In fact, I think that whatever has been going on between us—whatever this is—I think it's been going on for a long time. I think you're the reason I came here in the first place. I just didn't know it until now."

I didn't know how much I wanted to hear something like that until he said it. The floodgates opened and I dropped my head into my hands with a sob.

"Shh...don't cry."

"I don't know why I'm crying! I care about you, too, but I was just so confused. Dante said you were playing me. I hated you. And now this!"

He tried to pull his arms apart and bit back a cry. "Yeah," he panted. "My shoulder may be broken." He lay still for a moment. "Don't worry. We'll figure this out. But, first, I want to know what he's done to you. Did he touch you—"

"No! No, thank God!"

Dante hadn't gone there, thank goodness. The thought had crossed my mind that he would, especially when he'd thrown out that "let's get to know each other" comment.

Zander let out a long sigh. "I was so worried. I looked everywhere for you."

"*I* don't even know where I am, so how did you find this place?"

"Again," said Zander, "all I can say is that I just knew, or I guess I just felt where you were and followed my way here. I know that sounds really weird, but I can't explain it any other way."

Wow. Maybe that was one of his special powers or something. "Okay...Dante was right, you're gifted, too.

You must have abilities like him, like me...although I don't do anything special, just see in the dark..." I was rambling. I let that sentence die in the blackness between us.

There was a long pause.

Finally he spoke, and I let out the breath I was unconsciously holding. "I don't think that's my gift, although it's pretty cool—"

"So you have them!"

"Yeah, but...that's not what I do, at least until now."

"But you found me! You could tell what was wrong with me! That's not normal, right? Maybe you *find* people!"

"Tru, it's only ever happened with *you.*"

That shut me up. What did that mean? Only me?

He squinted. "Wait a minute. Did you say you could see in the dark? Because, that could be pretty useful right now." He tried to pull his wrists apart, but grunted in pain. "Damnit!" He breathed hard, through the pain. "My shoulder is really killing me. I can't do anything with it like this!" He tried to sit up again. "Agh!"

"Here, let me help you." I scooted closer, letting our hips touch, and helped him to sit up and lean against me, almost in my lap. We both paused to sigh loudly as that blissful hum enveloped us, blocking out the pain of our injuries for a moment.

"So not the way I imagined the next time in your arms," Zander said with a chuckle.

What the fried chicken? Did he just say what I thought he said?

When I remained silent, he tried to twist around to see me, which jostled his shoulder, causing him to suck in a ragged breath. "I don't suppose you could untie my wrists?" he asked.

Tears were leaking out of my eyes again. I wasn't sure if it was the gratitude that I wasn't down here alone, the "in each other's arms" comment, or that I could see how much he was hurting. Strangely, my shoulder was beginning to throb and I worried that I wouldn't be able to hold him up much longer.

"I'm so sorry you followed me here," I croaked, tears clogging my throat. Gently, I held his shoulder, afraid to cause more pain if I moved him to get to the rope around his wrists. I let my head lean into his, wishing that he was all better, that his shoulder was fixed, that we were both better and leaving this place. I just knew that he would have been able to get us out of here if he wasn't so injured. I sent a quick prayer up toward heaven to fix Zander.

"Tru—" Before he could say more, warmth spread from my fingertips. I gasped. Golden strings of light were wrapping around him, concentrating on his injured shoulder.

Zander's body clenched, and he unconsciously grabbed my leg just above my swollen ankle. I cried out as all the muscles in my body tightened and my teeth clenched.

When we both started breathing again, we were sprawled out on the floor and I immediately noticed Zander's hands were no longer tied. The rope lay off to the side, the bindings torn. He sat up easily this time and, with a quick rip, broke the rope wound around his ankles.

"What just happened?" I demanded. "How did you do that?"

Zander laughed, joy in his voice. "Awesome! Now I get it!" He reached out to me, feeling for my arm. As soon as he touched me, he smiled and looked into my eyes. *Looked into my eyes.* I realized he could see me.

"How? How can you see me?"

"I don't know, but when you touched me, like skin to skin, I started noticing the shelves across the room. I thought I was just becoming accustomed to the dark. But when you let go, the lights went out again. Tru, you are amazing!"

I smiled, not understanding where this was going, but grateful he seemed happy with me.

"What are you talking about?"

He rested a hand on my cheek. "Remember your hands at school? How they magically healed? Remember your arm in your backyard? How it healed?"

"What are you saying?"

"You! Tru! It's you! You healed me. You healed yourself!"

Was it possible?

"Okay," I said. "That would be a cool power." I thought about what Dante said I did for Bobby. Could it be true?

Zander laughed loudly, and then sobered, glancing toward the trapdoor. "And now, I'm going to kill that crazy bastard!" He stood up, pulling me with him. My ankle felt completely normal.

"He's not up there. He said he was going to the road to make a call. But that was a while ago. He could be back any second."

"Perfect!" Zander's grin was predatory. "Now you're going to find out what *I* can do."

He pulled me into his arms, hugging me tightly. I squeezed back, burying my face in his neck, enjoying the spicy scent of him. He pulled back and tilted my chin up.

"We have a lot to talk about, but I want you safe and as far away from this psycho as possible. Okay?"

"Okay," I agreed, drinking in his blue eyes and messy hair.

Then he let go of my arm. "Stand back there by that shelf."

"You can see it?" I asked.

"I remember where the door is."

"But, it's pitch black in here."

"Just stand back. I don't want you to get hurt if I knock something down."

I backed up to the shelf, unsure what Zander planned on doing.

With a grin, he leaped up toward the trapdoor. I gasped as he broke through and grabbed onto the edge of the floor. He pulled himself up and wrenched open the rest of the door. A second later, a long ladder was lowered down to me.

With a giddy exclamation of "Sweet!" I climbed out of the cellar.

Zander snatched me up as soon as I reached the floor. He ran his hands down my arms, then my sides and legs, confirming that I was indeed healed. By the time he looked me in the eyes again, my face was beet red. He laughed, cupping the sides of my face.

"I love the way you blush at everything." He further shocked me by dropping a swift kiss on my nose. "You really did it! You really healed us! You're amazing!"

There was so much I didn't understand, but being surrounded by my blue-eyed boy was one of the happiest moments in my life. However, it was over as soon as it started.

A car engine rolled up to the cabin. We pulled apart.

Zander kept me next to him as he quickly assessed the room. On the other side of the trapdoor, now just a ragged hole in the ground, sat a wood-burning stove and rack of fireplace tools. Zander ran over and grabbed the iron poker.

"Get behind the door," he whispered. We could hear footsteps approaching. I slipped across the room and flattened myself against the wall between the doorjamb and the window. Zander headed over to the door, lifting the iron poker.

28

Out of the Fire

Zander didn't give Dante a second chance to surprise him. When he stepped into the cabin, Zander was already swinging his weapon. But the guy had quick reflexes. He must have glimpsed something from the window. He ducked and rolled, missing a deathly blow by millimeters. Dante quickly scrambled to his feet, already reaching behind his back. He came up with a pistol before Zander could take another swing.

"No!" I gasped as Dante leveled the gun at Zander's head. His eyes radiated pure panic and I knew any hope of escape was disintegrating fast. I felt completely helpless and tried to move closer to Zander, but a small shake of his head stopped me.

"Don't even think about it, superman," warned Dante as Zander took a step. "Why don't you toss that stick of yours over there." He pointed to the left, away from me.

I met Zander's eyes for a second. Sadness. Regret. Disgust. He threw the rod against the far wall.

Dante laughed, still pointing the gun at him. "Wow. I totally wasn't expecting that. Seriously. You really surprised me. And look at you two!" He waved the gun between Zander and me. "You're all fixed up! How do you think that happened, I wonder? Well, I can't wait to find out, I must say."

"What do you want from us?" grunted Zander.

Dante's eyes darted between Zander and me. "She didn't tell you? Well, I suppose you haven't had that much time to catch up, being tied up and broken and unconscious... Anyway, you two are my golden tickets. I wonder how they'll classify you."

He tilted his head to the side, staring at us.

"I mean, you aren't anything I've seen before. I've been thinking, and I'm not sure if you're idimmu anymore. But whatever you are, the Collector is going to be extremely pleased. Which means he'll be extra nice to me!" His eyes sparkled avariciously. "By the way, how *did* you get out of my cellar?"

"You should have stayed away a little longer," Zander muttered.

Dante cackled. "Sorry about that. But I got everything tidied up quickly once I found a patch of cell service. The Collector was very interested in you two. To be honest, I've never heard him so excited about one of my catches. Yes, he's going to be very happy with me, especially once he learns who you are." Dante waved the gun at Zander. "I couldn't resist holding out on him about that." He cackled. "And to think I almost lost you. I really am lucky!"

I racked my brain for a plan. Obviously, Zander had some kind of super strength. Could he knock Dante unconscious before he did the same to him? Could I do something to Dante?

Zander inched toward Dante.

Dante narrowed his eyes. "Whoa, there. Not another millimeter. I'm so not messing around." His voice had gone deadly. "I'm a very good shot, and I'm okay with just bringing in one of you if it comes to that."

Zander raised his hands. "Whatever your boss is giving you, I can double it." He stepped forward.

Dante laughed and swung his arm over to me. "That's too funny! But I said, no moving! Either of you!" The gun was directed straight at my head, but Dante never took his eyes off Zander.

Suddenly I was so pissed. I mean, who did he think he was? I thought of my mom, how some stupid lunatic took her from me. No way was I going to let something like that happen again. With one last determined look at Zander, who seemed to be begging me not to move, I launched myself at Dante, the momentum throwing both of us toward the cellar.

At this point, my mind compartmentalized all three of our actions as if in slow motion. Dante noticed my attack a fraction of a second before I reached him. Zander moved toward us so fast, he was almost a blur. But he wasn't faster than the bullet. The gun went off.

"No!" Zander roared, grabbing at me as I sailed with Dante toward the hole in the ground.

Dante fell backward over the edge, one leg still on the floor and the other dangling over the hole. He grabbed at me, catching my hair while Zander snatched at my ankle. For just a second I was being pulled in opposite directions. With a painful rip, Dante fell backward, dropping head first into the pit.

Zander pulled me away from the hole, shaking and holding me tightly. "You okay?"

"I'm fine, I think." The back of my scalp stung. He must have pulled out a chunk of hair. I was probably bald on one side of my head.

"It's him we need to worry about," I said. He steadied me before letting go. We both peered down into the dark hole.

Dante lay in a halo of light, unmoving. The gun was still clenched in one hand, a chunk of blond hair in the other.

Zander rushed down the ladder, carefully lifting the gun from Dante's grip before he gained consciousness. He peered closely at the limp form, then up at me.

I knew before he said anything. I could see that Dante's neck was bent at an impossible angle.

"Don't touch him," I said. I could tell he wanted to check for a pulse. But we both knew he was dead. "We don't know if he can still zap you."

"I doubt it, but let's not test it." He climbed back up the ladder and pulled it up with him. "Let's get you home. I'll have Peter take care of this."

But I wasn't really listening. I had backed away from the cellar, pain spreading across my abdomen. I sat in a nearby chair, dazed. I pulled my hand away from my shirt as Zander stared at me. My hand came away covered in blood.

Zander grunted and touched his side as if in pain. Was he feeling my pain again? I could fix this, though. Closing my eyes, I pressed my hand against the wound again, wondering how I did it before. *Heal*, I thought. *Please, heal?*

He rushed over, hovering. "Tru, you were shot! But you can heal yourself, right? Like you did to us in the cellar!"

I shook my head, giving him a half smile. "It's not working, Zander. My cool power isn't working." I slumped in the chair, beginning to slide down to the floor. Maybe I was too hurt, maybe I couldn't heal from just anything.

Zander caught me, and carefully carried me over to the couch. He laid me out and lifted my T-shirt with shaking hands.

"It's bad, isn't it." My body began to tremble. "S-sorry," I bit out, teeth chattering.

"No!" Now Zander pressed his hand against the wound, staunching the blood loss. I gasped at the pressure, but then the wonderful hum we always felt took over, but more intensely than ever. Zander sucked in a deep breath.

"It must be the blood," I panted.

"Together," he said. "We'll fix this together."

"I don't know how."

"It worked before. Try again, Tru," he urged thickly. "Please," he begged. "I'm not going to lose you after everything we've been through. After all this time! I just found you! So try again, Tru, please." He leaned in closely. Was he crying?

"This feels so déjà vu." Now I was talking gibberish and maybe seeing things.

"Tru!" he whispered unsteadily. "Let's try together."

I lifted a hand to his cheek. "Okay." My voice was faint. "Maybe you did it. Maybe I just needed you." He leaned in the rest of the way, until our heads touched. The hum was now pulsing everywhere we touched. It was like a living, breathing force of nature. Our skin began to glow.

"Tru, I don't know exactly where we stand, but I do know that I want to get to know you better. I do know that I came here to find you. I know that there's a lot more going on than we understand, and I want us to figure it out together. I have so much to explain. So, you have to get better!" Zander insisted.

His heartfelt words seemed to do the trick. Heat pooled where his hand pressed against the wound. Suddenly, I felt a burning explosion, and as it reached my brain, my world went black.

29

Sirens

I OPENED MY EYES to my bedroom curtains rustling in the night breeze. Releasing a long sigh of relief, I sent a prayer of gratitude out into the great unknown. Thank goodness it was just a nightmare! Had I woken up Dad? I listened. Silence. A happy laugh escaped me as I swept back the covers and swung my jean-clad legs over the side of the bed.

Jean-clad legs.

I jumped from my bed and stared at myself in my mirrored closet doors. My hair was wild and tangled, my T-shirt ripped and bloody. My face had muddy streaks across it. I was filthy.

"No!" I groaned, collapsing to the floor.

"Tru."

I yelped and spun around.

"Sorry. I didn't mean to scare you."

Zander, equally disheveled, sprawled on my oversized beanbag in a corner. He ran his hands through his already spiky hair and stared inquiringly at me. He looked like he'd just woken up.

"You thought it was a dream, didn't you? I wish it was—except for the good parts," he said. He switched on the lamp next to him. Its soft glow spread across the room toward me.

My lips trembled against my fingertips. "Yeah." It had really happened. The ramifications were just starting to run through my mind. It was too much. I wiped the moisture from my eyes, determined not to cry.

"What happened?" I asked. "How did I get here? Does my dad know you're here?"

The beanbag made squishy sounds as he straightened out of it. He stepped over to me, squatting down on the carpet in front of me.

"Um, let's see..." he started, his voice low. "Your dad got home about an hour ago—he must have been working really late. But we were already here, which is a good thing because I don't know how I would have explained it. Anyway, I hid in your closet when he stuck his head in." He chuckled. "That's a first! Luckily he didn't look too closely."

He paused to peer more carefully at me. I ran a self-conscious hand over my fluffy hair, at the same time trying to remember if I had shoved any dirty laundry in my closet. I should have cleaned my room like Dad asked.

"And," he added, "I sent a text back to Ruthie that you were okay and you would explain everything tomorrow because there were a bazillion texts from her." He chuckled. "She almost came over here, but I said you were feeling sick and might be contagious. Hope that's okay."

"My phone! Oh good, then you found my backpack, too. You didn't say it was you, right?"

"No, she thinks the texts are from you. Why? She doesn't like me now? There's your backpack." He gestured to the corner of my room where the backpack sat. He pulled my phone out of his pocket. "And here's your phone."

"Thanks." I tucked it into my back pocket. "It's a miracle Ruthie didn't come over here anyway. I kind of told her what was going on."

"She knows?"

"Yep. After you and your brother mind-whammied me—"

"Mind-whammy?"

"Hey! That really hurt. And then you took off and pretended it all never happened..."

"Sorry. That probably hurt, too." He sighed.

"Well, anyway, I needed to talk to someone and she's my best friend."

"How did she take it?"

"Surprisingly well, but she thought that since your brother had these mad mind-warping skills, then you could be messing with my mind, too."

"That actually makes sense."

We stared at each other. He looked like a tornado victim, but there was strength in his eyes. His eyes said that although he understood, he wasn't messing with me. There was more, too, but I wasn't up to examining it.

"We both have a lot to figure out," I offered. "Maybe tomorrow things will make more sense."

I looked down at my bloody shirt. Had I really been shot?

"Don't worry about Dante. He won't hurt anyone ever again," Zander added. *Dante!* Something nagged in the back of my mind, something I had mulled over when I was stuck in the cellar. Then I remembered.

Dante had talked about how much I helped Bobby. Later, when I began to believe him, I wondered if I could help him, too. What was Dante like before he had been collected? What if I had tried? But as soon as I touched him, I would have lost consciousness. He thought I would hurt him. I had scoffed at the idea, but in the end that's exactly what I did. I remembered Dante's neck bent at a strange angle. Instead of helping him, I had killed him.

I covered my face, a sob escaping me. "I can't believe I killed him!"

"It was an accident, Tru. You know that, right?"

"But I pushed him on purpose. And he died!" I pressed my fingers into my eyes, hoping to block out the sight of Dante's bent body. I couldn't. It would be forever branded to my eyelids. I was a murderer.

Zander gently pulled my hands away from my face, but I didn't want to look at him. I didn't want him to see me.

"Tru, it was him or us. He shot you. It was self-defense. I would have killed him if I could have. You saved me. You saved both of us."

I finally looked at him, finally gave into that warm connection between us. If anything could make me forget tonight, it was that. I could get lost in his blue gaze. Something soared inside me when he looked at me like that. He seemed to notice the change in me. He let go of my chin, and my eyelids fell at the loss.

Zander cleared his throat. "I sent my brother after him. I brought you here and didn't want to leave before you woke up. I needed to make sure you were okay." He reached toward me again, but changed his mind, dropping his hand. "Are you? Okay, I mean?"

"Yeah," I said. Okay, but disappointed, I thought. Why wasn't he holding me like he had before? Suddenly I doubted my memories, my perception of our last conversation. Had it not happened like I remembered? Perhaps a bullet in the stomach could cause hallucinations. What about wanting to get to know me better? Had he really said that? People said all kinds of things in the heat of the moment. I ducked my face, embarrassed. I felt for the wound in my stomach. Everything was smooth. Nothing hurt. I wanted to lift up my shirt to check it out, but shyness prevented me.

"It's hard to believe," I murmured. "Did all of that really happen? Honestly, I don't know what to think." I looked up into his face, hoping he would understand what I was asking.

His lips thinned as he deliberated over what to say. He was quiet too long. I was tired of him squatting over me. I kneeled so that we were at eye level. Gathering up my courage, I rested my hands on his knees.

His eyes sparked bright blue and our breathing hitched. Tiny tremors rolled over our skin.

"What is that?" I asked.

His eyes darted down to my lips. Grabbing my hands, he hauled me up with him.

"I don't know yet, Tru. But whatever it is, it brought me here to you." He pushed me down until I was sitting back on my bed. Then he snagged my desk chair and straddled it backward, keeping several feet between us.

I lowered my eyelashes. He acted like he didn't want to touch me.

"Tru," he whispered, waiting until I looked back up at him. His smile of chagrin made him look bashful, which I had a hard time believing. "I can't think when you're touching me."

"Oh." I felt my cheeks reddening. "So," I soldiered on, "you came here to Scotts Valley the same way you found me at that cabin?"

"I think so, although at the time, I didn't realize I was searching for you. I just knew I needed to come here. I've been wanting to visit this area for about a year, actually since I was a kid, but this past year more than ever." He sighed. "Man, there's so much to tell you, there's no way I can explain it tonight." He looked at the alarm clock beside my bed. It read 12:00 AM.

"Okay, can I ask a few questions before you go?" I needed a few things answered tonight. The rest would have to wait until tomorrow.

"What do you want to know?"

"You say what I did was self-defense, but the police may not see it that way. What did your brother do with Dante?"

"Don't worry about it. He's not going to be found. You'll never have to worry about him again." He paused, staring at me. Worry lined his forehead. "Tru, it's not your fault. Besides, he shot you! You would have died."

I just nodded my head numbly. Of course I knew that. Of course I knew I didn't mean to kill him. I still took a life. Maybe I didn't need to, maybe I could have done something different. Maybe if I'd tried to help him instead...

"Thank you, Tru, for doing what you had to do."

Our eyes locked again and I hurt thinking of how close Zander had come to dying. I was happy he was alive.

I couldn't help wondering about Dante. I didn't know what his life was like before, what this "collector" had done to him. He had been mentally unstable for sure. He had hurt me, and I didn't understand his reasons or his motivations. But I suspected his behavior was manipulated and I couldn't hate him. I couldn't hate him for being insane.

Sanity was a fragile thing.

There was hate in my heart, though, directed at someone I didn't even know. Should I tell Zander his father was the Collector? What if Dante was just messing with me? I hated the Collector, whoever he was. Mixed in with that hate was fear. He knew about me. And he wanted to collect me. He would come for me. I knew it and it scared the crap out of me. But I wasn't going to wait for him to come for me. No, I would not go quietly. I would tell Zander what Dante said, but not right now. It could wait another day, right?

Zander watched the thoughts flit across my face, patiently waiting for a response. Oh yeah. He said I saved him.

"I think we saved each other," I replied. "When I heard you above in the cabin, it was the happiest moment of my life. I didn't think anyone would find me." I stalled there, wondering if I had said too much.

"I didn't tell my brother everything that happened."

My eyes widened. "Why?"

"I don't trust him."

"Why?"

"He doesn't like you."

"Why?" I sounded like a parrot. Zander smiled.

"He thinks you're a siren."

I stopped before I repeated myself. Zander was looking expectantly at me. I chuckled.

I took the bait. "O-kaaay... What's a *siren?*"

He looked a little overwhelmed.

"Wait," I said. "Dante mentioned sirens, I think, back at the cabin." That brought a scowl to Zander's face. "He also told me about akharus and usemis."

"Just akharu and usemi. You don't say the 's.'"

"Well, he told me about idimmu, too, these halfbreeds. They are known by other names, too, like sirens. He said I was one, but different. And that you are like me."

"A siren is a type of idimmu. A siren can force you to do or feel things that you don't want to. Peter thinks you are making me feel drawn to you."

"What?" I sputtered. "That's crazy!"

Zander laughed.

"I mean, I don't do that, do I?"

"Well, it certainly feels odd to constantly want to be near you. But sirens don't see in the dark or magically heal, so I'm guessing, no, you aren't. Besides, my friend Conrad has been researching this for me, and he doesn't think you're a siren. Idimmu usually only affect the mind. They can't physically change things, like you do when you heal. I've never heard of anything that can do what you do. Yeah, I know Dante made me unconscious, but I wonder if he just makes a person think they're asleep. I don't know."

My jaw dropped at his first words. He wanted to constantly be near me? It warmed me from head to toe because I wanted the same thing. It took me a moment to register the rest of his words.

"What? Then what am I? What are *we?* I remember in my dream that you and Conrad were talking about some prophecy?"

"Believe me, I've been wondering the same thing. I need to call him back. He was talking about some old legend that helped me figure out that I could find you just by opening up my senses. I didn't finish my conversation, you know, running through the woods, damsel in distress, evil villain, and all..." His mouth curved up on one side. "But I know now I can find you anywhere."

I giggled. "That could be a little annoying."

"Yeah, get used to it."

"Hey, what about me saving you?"

"Did I say damsel?" He laughed. "More like...what is the opposite of damsel anyway?"

Now he rested his chin on the back of the chair. My eyes felt watery and he sighed like he was giving in to something. I met him halfway as he lifted his head and leaned his chair forward, lightly rubbing his lips against mine. Then he withdrew, shaking his head as if to clear it.

"Maybe you are my own personal siren."

"Can guys be sirens?" I asked.

"I never heard of it, but who knows."

"Well, I think you're my siren, too."

We stared at each other for a while. Then we heard police sirens blaring in the distance. They got louder and louder, then faded away. I couldn't stand it. A girly giggle rose up in my throat.

"That was too weird," I said.

He chuckled. "Yeah."

"Maybe it was a warning. Maybe we're the type of sirens that warn people something bad is coming." I was such a pessimist.

"Or maybe we're the kind of sirens that tell people help is on the way."

I dropped my head to my chest. I wanted to hug him, but stayed where I was. What if he left? What if I couldn't handle whatever happened next? I had a lot more to tell him, but not yet.

"Guess we'll have to see."

"Tru."

I looked back up at him. We weren't touching, but I felt like we were. His eyes burned bright blue.

"It's going to be okay, Tru. I'm not going anywhere and I'm stronger than I look."

It was like he read my mind. He was strong. I remembered him leaping out of the cellar. Finding me against all odds. He wouldn't have done that if he didn't really care, right? I needed to change the subject. I cleared my throat.

"So, okay. Does Peter know what I can do, what you can do?"

After another meaningful look, he accepted the change in subject. "No, I don't think so. Although, I did mention your hands and your arm healing. But he thinks you just made me see that stuff. Like I said, I've never heard of instant healing. I thought that was just Hollywood imagination. And as far as my abilities, they aren't common to sethians or idimmu, either. My abilities have more in common with the usemi and akharu, but I'm not either of those. Anyway, let's just say I've been wondering what I am, too. What we are. We need to find someone who knows more. So far, all I've got is Conrad, but he's a genius and has access to the ancient archives."

"Sethians?" Great, another name. Was there a class for this stuff? Then I remembered that Dante mentioned it. "Oh, one of the three pure races?"

"Yeah. Sethians are my people. Well, at least I was raised sethian. I always thought I was one. But I guess

I'm not." His eyebrows squeezed together. "Anyway, sethians are a species of their own, created back in the days of Cain and Abel to protect humans and to enforce the laws over akharu and usemi. More recently, they enforce the idimmu, as well. I guess you could say they are all different species, related to humans, but not compatible, supposedly. For instance, akharu and usemi hate each other and sethians mediate between the two. Over the last several hundred years, the akharu and usemi populations have dwindled; they began mingling with humans, which is against sethian law because..."

"Mingling, as in..."

"Crossing the gene pools."

"Oh, I get it."

I was riveted, fragments of dreams coming back to me but none of it making sense. I was too exhausted to put the pieces together. The stress and excitement of the whole day was finally getting to me. I could really use Ruthie right now. She could probably make sense out of this—give me a "supernatural species for dummies" summary. A yawn escaped before I could stop it.

"Look," he said. "It's late. School tomorrow. Unless you aren't going?" He raised one eyebrow. "Might be a good idea."

I hadn't even thought about school. My friends, homework, and that whole part of my life seemed like another world away. It seemed unimportant compared to this new side of my life.

"I don't know," I answered honestly. I wondered if I would be able to leave the safety of my house. "Do I need to be worried about the Collector?"

"No," he answered firmly. "Peter and I are staying put and we'll be watching your back. You have nothing to worry about."

"But you just said you don't trust Peter. And he doesn't trust me. He thinks I'm 'controlling' you."

"I know. Don't worry. I'll convince him you aren't a siren. Besides, he's chasing another problem right now, one more important to him. He's not going to hurt you. I'll do most of the watching." He gave me lecherous smile.

I laughed. Were we flirting?

He was trying to derail me. But for some reason, I didn't quite believe Peter was suddenly on my side. Could I trust Zander? Whatever I was feeling about him, could it be blinding me? Could Zander really be subjective when it came to his brother? Again, I was too tired to think about it. I was safe tonight. This could wait until tomorrow.

"Okay!" I gave up. "I really want to hear more about these vampires and werewolves and people with cool powers. But I suppose I better get to bed. I don't know if my brain can hold much more tonight anyway, and I bet I need more than a few minutes to hear all about it." I rubbed my gritty face. "Ugh!" I'd forgotten how awful I looked. "I feel so gross!"

Zander just chuckled. "I'm feeling pretty grimy myself." He rolled his shoulders. "And I think that beanbag tried to swallow me. I feel like a truck rolled over me—"

As soon as he said it, regret showed on his face.

"Sorry, Tru. I didn't mean to—"

I knew he was thinking about my mother's accident then. I hadn't made the connection before he started backpedaling. But it reminded me about the real information I was dying to know.

"It's okay. One last thing," I said, finally looking back up. He raised his eyebrows. "Really, then you can go. I never got a chance to talk to you about what happened in my backyard." Zander groaned and set his forehead on the back of the chair. "I know those were werewolves, or usemi. And I know your brother tried to make me forget it."

"I'm really sorry about him. I tried to stop him."

"Yeah. I remember."

Zander looked back up at me. I locked him in my gaze.

"I was mad for a while, Zander, but I'm okay with it now. Just don't let him near me again. I'm still mad at *him.* He's an idimmu-sethian?"

"No, those are two separate species."

"Oh, so sethians can do mind-whammy things?"

"Well, not normally. It's a lot to explain. I promise to tell you later. But I'll handle him, don't worry."

"Anyway, I heard you and Peter talking about my mom's accident."

"Tru, I don't know much more than you do."

"But you sounded like you did! You said you were after the person—usemi? Whatever. You were after whoever hit my mom. So you know who did it."

"We suspect."

The thing was, I suspected, too. But I wanted to hear his side before I told him. There was so much to talk about. Another wave of weariness hit me.

Zander noticed. He stood up. "Let's get together tomorrow and talk about it, okay?"

I nodded. I realized I needed to sneak him out of the house. It hit me that I had a boy in my bedroom. Now I felt awkward, despite knowing that we were both feeling this need to be near each other.

"Let me make sure Dad is really out of it before you try to leave."

Trying to smooth down my wild hair, I got off the bed. Zander's hand stopped me, turning me around. One touch from him and I wanted to plaster myself against him. I resisted and looked up into his face.

"Hey, I, uh, just wanted to say you were amazing. What you went through would have sent most people into a mental institute trying to deal with it. But you handled it. Better than I would have, probably, if I were in your shoes."

I took a moment to compare myself, at this second right now, to me one year earlier. Back then I thought I was coma girl, but really I was some latent being, waiting to become something. Sure, I was something not quite human or normal by any means, but I was beginning to feel like I was something more amazing—undefined and untested to be sure, but amazing just the same. And with that knowledge, I was stronger and ready to do whatever it took to find my mother's killer. Look what I already accomplished. I experienced such great loss last year that I lost myself for a while. But I pulled myself out of that dark well in my mind, just as Zander and I had escaped the dark cellar at the cabin in the woods. I faced down my captor, I escaped death—more than once—and I discovered courage I never imagined possible. Darkness had nothing on me. I saw through darkness!

I liked this new person I was becoming. The old version of me was a sleeping me. I didn't know exactly what I was yet, but now I was *aware*—the sleeper had awakened. There was no going back.

Impossible, crazy beings existed, crazier than I ever was, too. I wasn't the only freak out there. Most importantly, I knew terrible truths and I wasn't losing it. And there were more to come. I felt the reality of that. I sensed a loosening in my mind where I had secrets wrapped up so tightly, I'd never examined them before. I was just noticing their existence. It was all coming out into the light. And I wasn't afraid. Tomorrow was coming whether I wanted it or not, and I would deal with it. But not alone. I didn't have to do it alone. I had my friends. I had my father. I had Zander and whatever was going on between us. I looked forward to discovering more. Hope bubbled up inside of me.

I stared into Zander's deep blue eyes, and felt power and confidence despite my dirt-streaked face. I loved the way his eyes sparkled, even in the dark. The light in them came from an inner strength, and I couldn't resist thinking that some of the sparkle had to do with me. I went up on my tiptoes. Like I knew he would, he met me halfway.

Be on the lookout for the next book in the *True Nature Series:*

Secrets of the Lore (Book 2)

Visit **karenlynnbennett.com** for deleted scenes, book lexicon, sneak peaks, news and more.

ABOUT THE AUTHOR

Karen Lynn Bennett grew up in a small farming town in central Washington with seven other siblings but has spent most of her adult life in northern California with her husband and two daughters. She finally went public with her secret writing life and now spends endless happy hours conjuring characters and plot lines. When she's not at her keyboard, she's brainstorming story ideas as she entertains her other hobbies—exercise, cooking, and traveling. Keep up to date with her books at ***karenlynnbennett.com***.